Some Predators Are Male

Miles Tripp

Some Predators Are Male

Miles Tripp

St. Martin's Press
New York

Library of Congress Cataloging in Publication Data

Tripp, Miles, 1923-
    Some predators are male.

    I. Title.
PR6070.R48S6   1986   823'.914   85-25203
ISBN 0-312-74348-3

First published in Great Britain by Macmillan London Ltd.

First U.S. Edition

10 9 8 7 6 5 4 3 2 1

PROLOGUE

Neil Pensom stood close to the entrance of an apartment block in south London and looked around. He didn't feel safe from attack and sudden disorientation. Someone unknown seemed intent on maneuvering him into extraordinary situations which had no imaginable purpose except to fill him with alarm and a sense of being viciously persecuted. To his knowledge he had no enemies. He was careful not to make enemies.

He pressed a bell by the entry-phone. A crackle from the amplifier was followed by a voice. 'Who is it?'

'Hello, Anthony. It's Neil.'

'My dear fellow, come on up. The door's open.'

With a last quick look around, Neil Pensom opened the main door. He had reached a temporary sanctuary, a place where he could put a bizarre sequence of events in order and decide whether to go for help to the police, a lawyer or a private detective. Or possibly he should go to a doctor because either a sick joke was being played on him or he himself was sick.

SOME PREDATORS ARE MALE
Part 1

Shandy closed the door, stared at her boss and asked, 'Why are you pulling a funny face?'

A flicker of irritation ruffled Samson's fat countenance. 'I wish you wouldn't barge in. It's good manners to knock.'

She advanced towards his desk with a sinuous movement. Samson, expert in body talk, recognised this as a danger signal. He became very alert. His defences couldn't have been sharpened quicker by a snake poised to strike.

'Good manners,' said Shandy with puzzled innocence. 'I thought when you hired me and showed me that tatty outer office with nothing but a clapped-out typewriter and an antique filing cabinet you told me to make myself at home. I thought at the time, thank God my home isn't like this.'

Samson knew he would probably lose the battle of wits. Shandy, whom he loved as though she were his daughter, usually bettered him in domestic argument. But, just as people who are accustomed to being losers end up by inviting loss because it becomes a familiar and therefore reassuring condition, he ploughed the old, sterile, stony field of defeat.

'What has making yourself at home in an office which was less than perfect when you arrived, but is now bristling with the latest high-tech, to do with lack of good manners?'

She laughed. 'One word processor, a telex machine and a computer link with a hacker-prone information bank – and you call that high-tech?'

'That computer is costing me the earth.'

'Well, we'll concentrate on your request to make myself at home. At home I don't knock on the door before going into a room. So, if I'm to be at home, why should I knock on your door?'

Samson moved his plough to more fertile ground. 'Very public school, very upper class, very professional.'

He waited for her reaction and wasn't disappointed.

'Professional? Upper class? I don't get it.'

'Very professional and upper class not to knock,' said Samson. 'Barristers barge into each other's chambers without knocking. Only the clerks knock. As for the upper class, do you think the Queen or Prince Charles knock before they go into a room? No. Knocking on doors is for servants. Ah, but of course, you're not my servant even if I am your boss and paymaster.'

She smiled and clapped her hands. 'Well done. You win. I'm just nothing more than a secretary-receptionist-telephonist-general-dogsbody.'

Samson shook his big head like an amphibian coming up from a long spell under water. 'You barged in for a purpose. Let's have it.'

Shandy leaned forward resting one hand on the edge of his desk and her long fair hair fell forward. She brushed it back with the other hand. This was a mannerism which had once annoyed Samson but now he was used to it, even liked it.

'I've got a Mr Pensom outside,' she said. 'He wants an urgent appointment. You're free. I wondered if. . .'

'What's his agony?'

'He wouldn't say. I did ask, but he wouldn't say. He must be the sort that believes in going to the top. Minions are for bypassing.'

'If it's another wife that's run away, I'm not interested. I'm sick of looking for runaway wives.'

Shandy wrinkled her brow. 'He doesn't look like a wife-chaser. A bird-chaser perhaps. Quite good looking.'

4

Samson considered whether to ask how a wife-chaser could be distinguished from a bird-chaser, decided not to, and said, 'All right. Show him in.'

'You still haven't told me why you were pulling a funny face.'

'If you must know, it wasn't a funny face. It was a thin smile.'

She gave an incredulous laugh. 'A thin smile? What were you smiling at?'

'I wasn't smiling at anything. I was practising. I don't sleep well, as I must often have told you, and last night in bed I broke the habit of a lifetime by reading a thriller about a private detective. This chap smiled thinly in most chapters and his smile was at its thinnest when he was facing an armed maniac. Well, my chances of being in the same situation are hopefully slender but as I have the same trade I thought I should practise the thin smile.'

'I shouldn't bother if I were you,' said Shandy. 'It makes you look as though you've got toothache.' She left his desk and moved towards the door. As she opened it, Samson, knowing he would be overheard by the waiting client, boomed out, 'Why can't I have a nice murder? All I ever get is missing people who don't want to be found.'

Shandy paused in the open doorway. 'Work on your smile,' she said. 'It's the detectives with the thin smiles who get the murder cases.'

Neil Pensom had a lean face which was almost handsome. A high forehead was topped by greying brown hair which looked as if it had been ruffled by a breeze and needed combing. But his eyes were his most striking feature. Brown and widely spaced they gazed warily out as if expecting the ambush of disillusion to be waiting round the next corner.

A man of many sorrows and acquainted with grief, thought Samson. He said, 'Please sit down.'

After a brief glance at the clocks hanging on the walls

Pensom selected a wheelback from a miscellany of chairs. He pulled it forward so that he was close to Samson's desk, but not so close that he could touch the desk. The chair was in the middle of a no man's land of worn Axminster carpet, and Samson found this positioning interesting. Usually clients remained where the chair was placed, preferring to keep a distance, but sometimes they brought the chair right up to his desk so that they could have close eye-to-eye contact. Such people were invariably male and self-assertive.

Pensom sat down, unbuttoned a dark brown blazer and rested a zipper-case on his lap. Fawn-coloured slacks, Samson noted. This client was very much a brown man. As a rule Samson liked adversary contact with potential clients if they were self-assertive men. It usually extracted more information from them than they intended. Moreover, the speediest way to obtain acceptance or rejection of his views on how the case should be handled was to lock horns early. But with Pensom he decided to take a softer line. There would be no thin smiles. Instead, he smiled naturally, showing an expanse of pink gum in which was set a row of perfect small white teeth.

'With this weather,' he remarked, 'I could use an air-conditioner in here. Take off your jacket, if you like.'

'No, thanks.'

'Have you come far?'

'Battersea.'

'That's not very close. Do you live there?'

'No. I've got an apartment in Dulwich. I'm staying with a friend.'

'Have you been there long?'

'Two or three days.'

'I meant, have you lived long in Dulwich?'

'Only a few weeks.'

Not a great communicator, thought Samson. 'I've got a flat the other side of Brixton,' he said. 'It's an interesting area. Constant change. Fine if you like variety; not so good if you like things to stay as they've always been.'

He waited for a response. There was none. He waited longer. In the silence, noises from the street below seemed amplified. Samson's office was in a district of south London where black and white, Indian and Chinese, Jew and gentile, Moslem and Christian, mingled colourfully on a circuit where cultural and racial fuses were permanently on an electric overload.

The silence became protracted.

The voice of a West Indian woman could be heard as she screamed, 'Where you goin'?' A car horn honked. Above, a jet airliner whined on its way to Heathrow.

Samson used silences. From them he could sometimes discover whether his client was impatient by nature or lacked self-confidence because both these types found an artificial hiatus like a vacuum which must be filled. But Neil Pensom waited patiently for Samson to speak and it was Samson who broke the silence.

'I realise you must have come to me for help of some sort.'

'Yes.'

'What sort of help?'

A flicker of amusement lighted Pensom's eyes. 'Not a missing person.'

'That's good. I'm bored with that sort of case.'

'Yes. I overheard.'

'I'm sorry.' Samson tried to look apologetic. 'I didn't mean it when I said I'd like a nice murder. Yours isn't a nice murder?'

'A sort of murder. I think someone is trying to destroy me mentally, and I want to find out who and why.'

'I see,' said Samson, but he didn't. Mental murder sounded symptomatic of paranoia and was a matter for a doctor qualified in psychological medicine, not a humble private detective. 'Are you sure I'm the right person to help you?' he asked.

'You are a private investigator?'

'I am indeed. A PI. "I" being first person singular, not, as is commonly supposed, "eye" meaning the organ of sight. Private eye' – he pointed at one of his own heavily lidded eyes – 'sounds like private spy but my business is investigation, not espionage.'

Neil Pensom gave no indication that this information was of the slightest interest to him. In a flat voice he said, 'I know it sounds melodramatic, but I'm convinced someone is either trying to drive me mad or playing cruel tricks on me. I want to know why. It can't be for money because I'm not a wealthy man. The opposite. It can't be the result of an emotional involvement; I don't have any. It can't be a family feud. I've no family to speak of. No brothers or sisters. One or two distant relations living in Cheltenham, that's all. My father died before I was born. My mother' – his voice became muted – 'died less than two months ago. There's no reason why anyone should want to persecute me.'

Not entirely a non-communicator, thought Samson. This man needed careful handling. He seemed on a knife-edge and the flat tone of his voice indicated depression. Samson reached for a notepad although in a part-open desk drawer a tape-recorder was already operating and registering everything said.

'Before you give me the facts there are one or two routine questions. Your name and present address will have been given to my secretary but I'd like to know your age.'

'Thirty-seven. . . . I began to go grey rather early in life.'

'And your occupation?'

'Production assistant with a television company.'

Samson pushed his notepad aside and put down his pen. 'Fill that out a bit,' he said. 'What does your work involve?'

'Most recently I've been looking for a location for a thriller serial.'

'Nothing to do with my job, I hope. It's really very boring. Nothing like one sees on the box.'

'No. The plot's about diamond smuggling. The story begins in Belgium, moves up to Holland, goes across the North Sea where we have a boat chase, and the rest is set in the east of England. Most of the stuff can be filmed over here but a few outside locations abroad are needed.'

Neil Pensom unzipped the case on his lap and took out a sheaf of papers.

'Is that the story?' asked Samson.

'No. It's my story. Perhaps I'm a writer manqué but I really wrote it to try to put events in order and perspective.' He reached forward and put the papers on Samson's desk. 'This can tell it better than I can.'

Samson looked at the papers as though they were undesirable insects. 'You want me to read that?'

'Yes, please. And then maybe you'd contact me and say what you think should be done.'

'I hate the phrase "Time is money",' said Samson; 'Time is nothing of the sort. It's the prime mover of the universe. It's God, if you like. But "Time is money" sums up what I must say to you. It's shorthand for the fact that I'm a professional man and require payment for reading your account of whatever it is.'

'That's fair enough. I'll manage to pay you whatever's the going rate.'

Samson leaned back in his swivel chair. 'My going rate is quite arbitrary. I don't belong to any professional body. If a case bores me, and I am easily bored, the costs are high. If it interests me, and it takes something very unusual to interest me, the costs are lower. I don't know as yet which category your case falls into.'

'I don't think it'll bore you. If you've come across something like it before I'll happily pay your top rate.'

'It'll cost you thirty pounds an hour to look at this and I should like an advance of that amount. My secretary will attend to that when you leave.'

'You should be able to read it within the hour but, if not, I'll gladly pay any extra.'

'That makes an agreeably interesting start,' said Samson. 'Most clients resent paying anything. They seem to think my services should be a State benefit. Were you recommended to me by a satisfied client?'

'I got your name out of Yellow Pages, actually.'

If ever there was a time for a thin smile and a sardonic comment, this was it. Samson missed his opportunity. He said, 'So Yellow Pages work after all. Congratulations. You're my first Yellow Pages client.'

'You will take on my case?'

'Until I know what your case is, I can't say.'

'But you will read my typescript?'

Samson nodded. 'I will.'

'When can I expect to hear from you?' Anxiety pencilled fine lines across Pensom's forehead.

'I'll read it as soon as possible.' Samson glanced at his watch. 'I might even take my lunch here and read it then.' He paused. 'It might help,' he said, 'if you'd give me some idea of the problem. In a couple of sentences, what's it all about?'

Pensom shifted on his chair so that he could grip each side of the seat with his hands. It looked as if he was afraid that without support he might fall off and was the action of someone under an extreme degree of tension. 'Couple of sentences. That's not easy.'

'You did mention a sort of mental murder,' Samson remarked.

'I've been forced into situations where people treat me as though I'm somebody else. It seems like a deliberate attempt to destroy my sense of identity. That's what I mean by mental murder.'

'Have you any idea why this should be? Why you should be treated like this?'

10

'That's what's so disturbing. There's no consistency in the character being imposed on me or in the type of situation involved. There's no theme. No rationality. It's like a nightmare where a friend you're speaking to suddenly becomes a menacing stranger and instead of being in the safety of your home you're in the middle of an unknown and hostile country. It may not sound much but when you read my account I think you'll understand.' Pensom's grip on the chair slackened and in a more vibrant voice he said, 'And in case you think I may be a victim of amnesia of some sort, I'm not.'

'That thought did pass through my mind.'

'I have not lost my memory, or any part of it, Mr Samson.'

Samson inclined his head. 'All right. I accept what you say. . . . You've no idea who would wish to do this to you?'

'I wouldn't be here if I had.'

'No enemies?'

Pensom gave a shy smile. 'I like to think people like me.'

'Have you many friends?'

The smile vanished and Pensom looked uncertain. 'Not a lot of friends, no. Until she died I spent most of my spare time with my mother. It hit me hard when she died.'

Samson's early life had been tough. Although he could feel sympathy for underprivileged races or communities he was not very sympathetic towards individuals unless they suffered from a severe mental or physical disability. 'It must have been dreadful,' he murmured and hoped it sounded sincere.

'Yes.'

'And you don't want to talk about the problem until I've read about it.'

'That's right.'

'Is there anything else you'd like to say while you're here?'

'Not really. . . . I would like to know what you think

11

should be done, as soon as possible. It is urgent. I expect everyone says that, but it's true. You'll understand when you've read that.' He nodded towards the typescript.

Samson stood up and it was apparent that a large body was supported by short legs. Stores that sold ready-made suits never received his custom. 'I'll read it as soon as I can,' he said, and extended a hand from a tailor-made sleeve. 'I'm glad Yellow Pages introduced us.' He pressed a concealed button with his knee. 'My secretary will show you out.'

Summoned by a red light blinking on her desk Shandy appeared at the door.

'Show Mr Pensom out, will you, my dear? He's kindly agreed to make a payment on account.'

'Certainly.'

Samson sat down and reached for the sheaf of papers. The text was typewritten and the opening sentence looked promising. The scene was Antwerp, and Samson, who enjoyed wandering around harbours gazing at ships at anchor, liked Antwerp.

When Shandy reappeared she said, 'First it's the thin smile; now it's calling me your dear. What's got into you?'

Samson looked up. 'I'll tell you what hasn't got into me. Coffee and some ham rolls. Throw in a couple of hard-boiled eggs. And a nice gateau to follow. I'm eating here today.'

She gave him a disapproving look. 'A nice salad would be much better for you.'

'Maybe. I'll change that order. Make it a bottle of hock instead of coffee. It's too hot for coffee. And try not to disturb me. I've got some reading to do.'

'What sort of reading?'

'This. Half a book. By a man whose identity is being attacked.'

In some lights and at some angles Shandy had the type of beauty that had made Garbo attractive. The light and angle were right as she stood, one hand on hip, and said,

'Identity crisis? That's a shrink's job.'

'Right. And if I think he needs that sort of help I shall tell him so. . . . By the way, did he give you thirty pounds on account?'

'Yes.'

'In that case,' said Samson rather wearily, 'I've got no option but to read this stuff.'

I needed only two days in Antwerp to line up locations. On the morning of the third day, with time in hand, I decided to take a look at Rubens House and, if waking nightmares have a start — sleeping nightmares usually have such horrific ends we forget how they began — my waking nightmare began in the studio that Peter Paul Rubens built as part of his house some three hundred and fifty years ago.

As I wasn't part of a conducted tour I wandered round the house in a random way and had already glimpsed the great studio from a small gallery room known as the Tribune. It looked cold and bare, a shell which had once been filled with vivid canvasses and panels; patrons and pupils; life noise and colour. On entering I immediately noticed a painting of two naked bodies. The man, stomach sucked in, seemed to be lecturing a woman who leaned against a tree. It was the artist's famous juvenile work, *Adam and Eve*.

I was about to move on when a woman's voice said, 'What do you think of it?'

I turned. She was obviously speaking to me.

If I was writing this for commercial profit, and not to put on record a weird sequence of disordered events, I would make the woman young and beautiful. She was not. She was older than me and solidly built. Her hair was iron grey and looked like a wig. There was nothing out of the ordinary about her face except that on her left cheek was a huge brown mole. Three long, stiff, black hairs sprouted from it.

'You can see the old boy fancied the plump ones even

13

when he was starting,' she said and laughed.

In my job I sometimes have to make small talk but I wasn't on duty and didn't feel like making small talk with a stranger. So I simply said, 'Yes.'

'Adam and Eve. Genesis. A beginning. Love and life. I think it's wonderful, don't you?'

I couldn't think of anything to say, and so said nothing.

'I should have been born in Rubens' time,' she went on. 'Nowadays people like me are at a discount.' She thrust one leg forward, stuck out her chest, threw back her head, and in a sort of growl said, 'How about this, Peter Paul?' She held the odd pose for a moment before returning to normal stance. 'I hope I'm not embarrassing you,' she said, pulling a serious face.

Her English was perfect but she spoke with an accent I couldn't place.

'Don't look so hunted,' she continued. 'There's no need for it. But you should know that.'

I didn't know what she meant, and said so.

'I'll bet you dislike being accosted by women.'

She was grinning at me as if daring me to say, 'Yes, I do. Push off.'

I funked it. I said, 'The studio and house have been well preserved.'

'Well preserved? You make the place sound like an old man who's still got a vestige of good looks.' Then she said something utterly incomprehensible. She said, 'Shall we pretend we don't know each other. I'm Amanda.' She thrust out a hand. Reluctantly I shook hands but she hung on to mine, squeezing it so that the handshake was like an intimate greeting between old friends.

'And you?' she enquired.

'Me.' I extricated my hand.

'Your name,' she whispered, leaning forward.

I told her. I wish I hadn't. But I was off balance and I've never found it easy, on the spur of the moment, to be abrupt or impolite with a woman.

'I like Neil,' she said. 'It's manly and I do like manly men.' She glanced at the picture. 'I'll bet Adam was a real man. Well, he must have been, mustn't he? Yes, I like Neil.'

My classics master used to say, 'Neil desperandum, my boy, but by God you make me despair.' From that time I have disliked my first name and I didn't like it any better when repeated by this odd woman.

Then she toyed with my surname. 'Pensom,' she said. 'That's strange.'

Why was it strange? I didn't ask. Instead, I looked at my watch, and not in a surreptitious way either.

'Good heavens,' she exclaimed in a deep voice. 'Is that the time? I must go.' And then, in a normal voice. 'Is that what you're going to say?'

In fact, it was. And, as I'd had enough, I said, 'I do have to go, Mrs . . .'

'I'm Amanda. Remember?' And then she said the most extraordinary thing I have ever heard from a woman, or from anyone. She said, 'I didn't tell you my other name because you really ought to know it. It's the same as yours.'

At that point I fled, pursued by her laughter.

I couldn't get to my hired car fast enough and because I was unfamiliar with its controls very nearly had an accident. I was many kilometres from Antwerp, and had crossed the border into Holland before I'd fully recovered my poise. I'd been badly disturbed by the woman. If I'd thought she was mentally ill I would have felt sorry for her but no more. But I didn't think she was crazy. It was the things she said that were crazy.

Samson put down the typescript and gazed at one of the clocks hanging on the wall of his office. It was an antique tavern clock with a dial disproportionately large by comparison with the pendulum case below. Perhaps because its physical construction was similar to his own it was one of the favourite clocks in his collection and when he wished to concentrate he would sometimes sit staring at its moon-like face with its hands permanently splayed at twenty minutes past eight.

He had paused from reading to consider the style of Pensom's story. With its snatches of dialogue and descriptive passages it resembled a novel and anyone could easily be beguiled into treating it merely as an entertainment. But how else should it be treated? As the case history of someone obsessed with questions of identity? Evidence of a conspiracy to destroy a man's sanity? A puzzle in which the author had unconsciously inserted clues which might provide a stranger (or a private investigator) with insight into the motive, and possibly the identity, of a persecutor?

The last alternative seemed most likely. But to arrive at this insight it would be necessary to understand the character of the person telling the story. If a reader could find out what made Neil Pensom tick, it might lead to the person who wanted to disrupt that ticking and make him purposeless as the tavern clock. Pensom had said that the written word could tell of his predicament better than any oral explanation, but Samson guessed there were other reasons for writing the story. He opened a desk drawer, switched on a dictaphone and picked up its microphone.

'The Antwerp sequence,' he began. 'First, why with time to spare did he go to Rubens House? Is he an art lover? Many other places of more popular interest could have been visited in the time available. The magnificent Brabo fountain, for example, or the zoo. I would have chosen the splendid clock in Central Station. Why Rubens House? Is he an artist manqué as well as a writer manqué? Or was he simply interested in seeing a famous picture of a nude couple?'

Samson paused from dictating and, after a few moments' thought, put down the microphone.

* * *

16

Except for the sign 'Douane' there was no evidence of a customs check on traffic. I sped through at about 90 k.p.h. The roads were fairly straight, occasionally lined by poplars, and the land very flat. Hundreds of acres (or hectares) have been allocated to the production of crops of sugar beet, maize and spinach. I liked the flat, open countryside; it reminded me of childhood holidays with Mother in Norfolk; and by the time I reached the ferry at Breskens I felt completely relaxed. The encounter with the peculiar woman was nothing more than a bad memory.

Every twenty-five minutes a ferry plies between Breskens and Flushing (or Vlissingen as the Dutch prefer to call it) and the trip across the West Scheldt takes about twenty minutes. It would be from here, either Breskens or Flushing, that the diamond smugglers would embark for their journey across the North Sea. It was up to me to decide which of the two towns should be the take-off point, but, having read up their histories and amenities before leaving England, I was in no doubt which I should select. I had told GLJ as much and although he had been keen on a dike and a polder – helicopters and all that – the impracticalities had been obvious and he had settled for either Breskens or Flushing.

Breskens, to my mind, had little to commend it except as a pleasant but unremarkable holiday report. Flushing, on the other hand, although having an industrial complex also possessed a fine boulevard and good hotels. And it had a history. It was from here that Philip II of Spain sailed after having been rejected by the Dutch.

Unfortunately as I arrived at the ferry departure point a ferry was just leaving. This meant I would have to wait a short while. Parking my car near the head of the queue for the next ferry I went to a modern single-storey restaurant which relied on travellers for custom. Fruit and chocolates were on sale at an outside stall and as the peaches looked delicious I bought one.

17

I was paying for it, and congratulating myself on having the foresight to acquire guilders before leaving Belgium, when a voice behind me said, 'Heavens above! Are you following me or am I following you?'

I turned. It was that pushy woman again. My heart sank.

'A peach,' she said, 'that's not a very manly fruit. Most Adams prefer apples.' She laughed. 'Don't look so scared. I'm not going to snatch your peach away. I'm only joking.'

Joking? What was funny about it?

'Where are you going?' she asked.

'I'm going on the next ferry.'

'Don't be silly. Where are you heading for?'

I thought quickly. When I had been discussing locations with GLJ he'd fancied a particular polder called Vrouwen-polder. It was where a huge curving dike separated two expanses of water. Luckily I remembered its name.

'I'm on my way to Vrouwenpolder,' I said.

She frowned. 'I don't know where that is.'

I had a map in my pocket and pulled it out. But it was difficult to unfold with the peach in my hand and, before I could stop her, she had taken the peach.

'I'll hold this for you,' she said. 'Don't worry, I'm not going to eat it.'

I disliked the idea of her handling my fruit but there was nothing I could do about it. I unfolded the map and indicated Vrouwenpolder. 'It's here,' I said, 'on the way to Goes.'

She smiled. 'I'm going that way. I'm aiming for Bergen-op-Zoom.'

I said, 'Good.' I meant, 'Good. I can lose you when we disembark at Flushing. You'll go to the polder on your own.'

An angry red-faced man appeared and said something to me in Dutch. I recognised him as the driver of a car that had arrived just ahead of me. 'I'm sorry,' I said. 'I can't

18

speak Dutch. I'm English.'

In fairly good English he said, 'I've been using this ferry for three years and it's never left before time. Today it has to leave ahead of schedule. I'm going to lodge a complaint. Someone will pay for this.' Scowling, he stomped off.

'How rude of him to interrupt us,' said the woman. 'No manners at all.' Having delivered this criticism she put my peach to her mouth and took a savage bite out of it.

'That's my peach,' I exclaimed.

She looked at the fruit, its flesh torn and juice trickling down her fingers. 'So it is.' She threw back her head and laughed. 'How stupid of me. I'll buy you another.'

'It doesn't matter.'

'I would like to.'

'It doesn't matter,' I repeated, and I know my voice was overloud.

'There's no need to be cross,' she said. 'It was an accident.'

'I realise that.'

'Good.' She took another bite. 'I might as well finish it now that I've started – unless you would like to?'

'No, thank you.'

Between mouthfuls she said, 'I expect you're wondering what I'm doing in Holland.'

'No.'

'I'll tell you then.' She wagged a sticky finger at me. 'I'm looking for my husband. I know he's over here somewhere. Why are you looking at me like that? I didn't say I was looking for *a* husband. Silly man. I'm looking for *my* husband.'

She paused as if expecting a response from me. I had nothing to say.

'At the same time,' she went on, 'I'm exploring Holland. I've always had a thing about the Low Countries. My mother came from Ghent.'

I wished the next ferry would hurry up and arrive. As it

19

was, I had to listen to a diatribe about a daughter who, like her husband, had gone astray, but I can hardly recall a thing she said except that, like me, he was younger than her.

When the ferry swanned in like a dowager arriving late at a ball I felt an immense sense of relief.

'See you on board,' she cried as I sped to my car.

Again, on board, I recall little of what was said. I do remember it was a fine afternoon. The sky was clear and there was plenty of shipping on the river. At one stage, however, I thought I would go mad with frustration. She had pinned me against a railing and when I tried to move she blocked me. I was obliged to stand in close proximity. It was an awful experience and I had difficulty in averting my gaze from the hairs which bristled from her mole. They seemed to have a life of their own, independent of her face.

When we disembarked at Flushing she called out, 'See you at the polder.'

It was easy to lose her car and soon I was aiming for the waterfront. My aim was to find a hotel close to the river. It wasn't long before I found a suitable place. It was so close to the Scheldt I felt I could reach out and touch the ships passing by. I parked my car in a side street and got out.

I noticed a grey van pull up in front of me. Three men jumped from its back and as I walked by they grabbed me and bundled me into the van. Something hard was pressed against my ribs. One of the men said, 'You won't talk or move if you know what's good for you.' It sounded like a line from one of GLJ's thrillers, but it wasn't. Again my ribs were jabbed with what I guessed was a gun.

We travelled in silence and it was hard to see the faces of my captors in the shadowy interior of the van. Eventually, after some time had passed, two of the men began talking in a foreign language. Then I was told to close my eyes. A blindfold was fastened across my eyes and very soon the van came to a halt. I was helped from the back and led a

20

few yards. I was guided up three or four steps and into a confined space. My sense of smell is good since I gave up smoking and I noticed a smell of diesel fuel and the staleness of an ill-ventilated room. I wondered if I had been put aboard an aircraft. Then I was pushed against yielding material and told to sit. The blindfold was removed and an engine started.

I was seated on a bunk inside what turned out to be a big freight truck, a juggernaut. Much of its interior had been converted into a windowless room with a table and chairs in the centre, a radio transmitting and receiving set in one corner and a video monitor close by. And as I looked around I realised I was in a mini-studio, brilliantly lighted. The truck must have been equipped with some powerful batteries. Two small fans set into each of its sides provided the only ventilation and the room was oppressively warm.

The vehicle moved forward and began to accelerate. My captors were an oddly assorted bunch. The man who seemed to be the leader was sallow faced, almost bald, and wore thick-lensed spectacles. The man who had kept the gun at my ribs was a huge fellow with a mop of black hair and a bushy black beard. Dressed in the right gear he would have made a superb pirate. The third man was younger than the other two and was a fresh-faced, flaxen-haired youth. His shirt was open to the navel and he wore a silver medallion round his neck. I never learned their names but mentally called them 'Seedy', 'Beard' and 'Medal'.

They looked at me. I looked at them. I asked what the hell all this was about.

Medal positioned himself behind a tripod-mounted camera.

Seedy said, 'Say that again.'

'What the hell is all this about?'

I realised that sound and vision were being recorded. But for what conceivable purpose? I decided to make it clear I was being held under duress. I forget my exact words but they were on the lines of the strongest possible protest at this interference with my liberty. I would complain to the authorities, demand compensation, etc. etc.

Seedy waited until I'd run out of steam and then said, 'You English have a great sense of humour. We do not acknowledge the authority of undemocratic systems.'

He made a remark to Beard in a language I didn't understand. Beard laughed.

I have a good knowledge of French, some Italian and a smattering of German but that is the limit of my linguistic ability. I sensed they were speaking in Russian and I asked where they came from and why I was being treated in this uncivilised way.

'I ask the questions,' said Seedy, coming to sit beside me so that we were both on camera. 'But as an agent yourself I am surprised you should ask why you're being treated this way. After all, it's precisely what your crowd did to Stanislaw.'

I told him I hadn't the faintest idea what he was talking about. The name Stanislaw meant nothing to me; I was not an agent; I was a television production assistant.

He nodded. 'Yes. A good cover. Better than the usual salesman-abroad line. That cover is becoming over exposed.' He paused and chuckled. 'Over-exposed. That's a joke. A pun.' He waited for amusement to dawn on my face but when he saw not the slightest twitch of a smile he continued, 'Television. Yes. That's neat. You can go anywhere and ask anything. Unfortunately for you, your cover was blown last week in a Hamburg hotel by someone who is far too fond of the ladies. If I say "Charlie" you'll know who I mean.'

'The only Charlie I know,' I said, 'is a floor manager and he's gay.'

'Gay? Carefree and merry? Well, let us skip the jokes and get down to hard business. I recommend you to tell the

22

truth. You are not in television, are you?'

'If you doubt my credentials, I can tell you everything about television colour production including such things as colour separation and Quantel.'

'I would expect you to,' replied Seedy. 'You wouldn't be much good as an agent if you hadn't perfected your cover.'

'It isn't a cover. Look at my passport.' As I spoke I realised that my passport and belongings were in the car I'd hired in Antwerp.

'We have your so-called passport,' said Seedy. 'We have taken everything from your car which could identify you. You are now without identity. Stateless. A non-person.' He shook his head. 'For an agent you aren't very smart. You walked into our hands. Your wife was more clever.'

This was becoming a black farce. I almost laughed as I said, 'This is ridiculous. I'm not married. I haven't got a wife.'

'Don't treat me like a fool, Mr Pensom. Your wife gave us the slip. She must have suspected something and went off in a different direction. This meant we couldn't take both of you as we would have wished.'

'You've obviously got the wrong person,' I said, trying to keep my cool. 'I'm a television production assistant and I'm not married. I don't know what you're talking about.'

Seedy adjusted his spectacles which had slipped forward on his nose. Then he took them off and polished the lenses on a rather grubby handkerchief. When he had replaced them he peered closely at me. 'I'm looking at a man,' he said, 'who would deny his wife her proper status. What is she then? Your mistress?'

I had to smother rising anger. It would do me no good to lose my temper. 'I haven't the foggiest idea who you're talking about.'

'I'm talking about your companion in the art gallery and on the ferry, of course. Who else? Or are you like Charlie and lose track of wives and mistresses.'

23

'That woman isn't my wife. I'd never seen her before today when she struck up a conversation with me.'

Seedy gave his giggling chuckle. 'Never saw her before! Come on, Mr Pensom. You were seen holding hands in the gallery and on the ferry-boat you were huddled together like lovebirds.'

'This is absurd. She means nothing to me. She's a tourist . . .' I broke off at this point because I'd remembered something she'd said.

'A tourist,' Seedy prompted.

'She told me she was exploring Holland *and* looking for her husband. Not *a* husband, *her* husband. She was sure he was somewhere in the Low Countries.'

'You don't expect me to believe that?'

'It's what she told me.'

'An attractive woman like that searching in Holland for a lost husband?' Seedy made it sound as improbable as a gazelle hunting for a lion. 'You find her attractive, do you not?'

'No, I don't,' I said flatly, and I looked at the camera as I spoke. Let them make this a close-up. 'I do not find her in the least attractive.'

'Strange. In my country women of her physique are much admired. . . . But we must get back to the main business. Why were you taking photographs in Antwerp of places connected with the diamond industry?'

'Because this was needed for the film I'm working on.'

'And what is this film about?'

'Diamond smuggling.'

Seedy crashed his fist into the palm of the other hand. A gesture of triumph. 'Exactly. Diamond smuggling. At last we are getting to the truth. You are involved in spoiling the diamond trade between my country and South Africa. Admit it.'

'I admit nothing of the sort.' Although I spoke with spirit, I was getting very nervous. Where were they taking

24

me? To Russia? Would I end up in Lubyanka? Perhaps I shouldn't have said anything once filming started. I've known clever editors stand truth on its head and make liars of honest men.

'According to our information,' Seedy continued, 'your instructions were to meddle with the sale and delivery of industrial diamonds. As you must know, the present trading is under spot market prices and this is connected with Spanish wheat.'

I had never heard such rubbish and said so. If I hadn't been an unwilling captive I would have laughed at something so ludicrous. None of it made sense and I know nothing about undercover trading between the Soviets and South Africa and Spain. I know, as everyone else does, that behind the posture of governments a good deal of traditional barter exists and what is said in public bears no relation to transactions that occur *in camera*. This is called pragmatism, a euphemism for self-interested expediency.

'So. It is rubbish, is it?' my interrogator asked.

'Absolute rubbish.'

Seedy turned to the young cameraman and said something which clearly meant 'Cut'. Then the three men sat round the table, a pack of cards was produced and they began playing a three-handed game I didn't recognise. I reckon to know most card games but this one didn't seem to be a gambling game and perhaps that's why I didn't recognise it.

There was no chance of making a getaway while they were occupied with cards. Beard was seated facing me and his eyes kept flicking up to look in my direction. Apart from this, the vehicle seemed to be moving at some speed. But the break gave me an opportunity to assess the situation. Every so often my mind would flash back into the past seeking a link with it and my present predicament. I could find no connection.

My father had died before my birth and I had been

brought up by my mother, a lady of strong will and principles. My father had left her well off and I was sent to an expensive preparatory school where the accent was on religious education and military drill. Our drill instructor was a man in his seventies who had served in the First World War and he instructed us endlessly on how to dress from the right – 'As you were, you 'orrible little boys' – and how to form fours. What with having to learn the Sermon on the Mount by heart and a World War One freak it's a wonder I'm as normal as I am. But on the credit side, I had an aunt, Mabel, who was sympathetic to my ambition to be involved in some way with the theatre. I found the idea of working behind the scenes at a theatre very alluring. I think I would have liked to act but was rather too self-conscious in those days and suffered from stage fright.

I don't know how Aunt Mabel persuaded Mother to let me join a repertory company, but she did. I was paid four pounds a week and nobody belonged to Equity or any other union. It was a rather amateur outfit and for my four pounds I was call-boy, tea-boy, given walk-on parts when a crowd scene needed to be suggested, and assistant to the assistant stage manager who herself doubled as prompt. It was chaotic and great fun. Like everyone else who has had stage experience I've got a fund of stories of entrances muffed, disasters with special effects, and so on, and when I look back on this period in my life I realise I have never been happier even if there were bad times when there wasn't enough in the kitty to pay our wages.

In time the company folded. I joined another, more prosperous and professional, which had a decent booking list. It was while we were playing in Birmingham that I got a big break, purely by chance. I was trapped in a faulty elevator for fifteen minutes with a television executive. As a result of our conversation I got a job on the production team and thus a foothold in the industry to which I am glad to belong. Since my start in television I've been fully employed and acquitted myself reasonably well. But nothing in this past life gave me the slightest clue to why I should be abducted.

In all honesty I should say that while reviewing my life as I sat on a bunk in a claustrophobic juggernaut, my thoughts sometimes turned to Marler, who is a part of my life I bitterly regret. I wished to God I had never met the man, although he wasn't a man when we first met; more a youth, and not unlike Medal in looks. He is utterly ruthless and yet can't stand the sight of blood. Yet he won't hesitate to have blood shed, and metaphorically he is a bloodsucker. But as I watched the mysterious card game it struck me that ironically I was safe – safe from Marler. I found myself thinking 'It's an ill wind that blows no good' and 'Every cloud has a silver lining'. And I consoled myself with the knowledge that Mother never knew of my problem with Marler. She was spared that. I think Aunt Mabel would have understood. She wasn't as inflexible as Mother. In fact she was something of a diplomat. I'll never know how she persuaded Mother to let me go into repertory.

Of course, I wasn't simply recalling the past, I was trying to fathom out why I should have been captured. It must be a case of mistaken identity, I decided. Perhaps I bore a physical resemblance to a known British agent and had been grabbed in error. But how did someone called Amanda fit into this picture? She had said one or two things which hadn't made sense. Had she too thought I was someone else? Did I have a *Doppelgänger?*

The game of cards finished abruptly as if all three had suddenly got bored with it. Seedy went to the radio set. He spoke what I assumed was Russian into a microphone and after listening to a response for some moments took off headphones and turned to me.

'Soon you will be transferred to a car. If you wish to use the toilet, there's a portable lavatory in the rear. My comrade will show you. But don't try anything foolish.'

Beard took me past the camera and through a door. He indicated a small closet. 'Mind your head as you step through,' he advised.

It was like the door in an aircraft, only with less headroom and it had the customary attachment indicating whether vacant or engaged. If the truck was purpose built, as seemed likely, it could hardly have been built for use in Russia. I have never been behind the Iron Curtain but I can't believe English is the lingua franca for loo occupation.

The faint singing of the juggernaut's tyres on a hard surface was clearly audible – the studio must have been fairly well soundproofed – and I guessed we were moving fast. And then I heard the wail of a police siren. My heart leapt. Was the truck to be intercepted? If so, and if it came to a halt, I would remain in the loo, with door locked, and shout for help. Hope was short lived. The police car swept past and its wail faded in the distance. I toyed with the idea of staying locked in the loo but decided against it. The beefy Beard would kick down the door and I should get roughed up for my pains.

A light rap on the door and Shandy entered carrying a tray. Its only content was a plate of fresh salad. Lettuce, sliced tomatoes and cucumber lay in the centre and sprays of watercress garnished the edge. The salad was topped with three walnuts.

'What's that?' asked Samson, eyeing the plate with disfavour.

'Your lunch.'

'I didn't order that.'

'This is better for you. With your eating habits and weight you're asking for a coronary and I don't want a dead boss; I'd be out of a job.'

'I like your honesty.'

'You know it's time to turn over a new leaf and you could do worse than make it a lettuce leaf.'

28

Samson sighed. 'Put it down. It's decorative.'

She placed the plate on his desk and laid a serviette, knife and fork beside it. Samson peered at the empty tray. 'I can't see any drink or is that restricted too?'

'Sorry. Forgot. I'll fetch it.' She made no move to go. 'What's it all about?' she asked, pointing at the open typescript.

'Hard to say, as yet. It's written with hindsight. It's been carefully put together. I have a feeling there's been a selective process and, in its limited way, selection makes a work of art, not a spontaneous statement. I'm not sure who it's been written for. It's something more than putting one's thoughts in order.'

'Can I read it?'

'I'd like you to, when I've finished. But first, would you find out who GLJ is. I'd guess these are the initials of a television director or producer responsible for sending Pensom to Antwerp.'

'Find out who GLJ is? I'll try.' She took a walnut from the salad and popped it in her mouth.

'You can have the lot,' muttered Samson.

'As a matter of interest, is there any reason why you shouldn't ask Pensom who GLJ is?'

'I don't want to call him every few minutes with a new question.'

'OK. . . . It might help if I knew why he was being sent to Antwerp.'

Samson told her what he knew of the TV storyline about a diamond-smuggling operation.

'Right,' she said. 'I'll make a start.'

'And don't forget the wine.'

When she had left the room he contemplated the salad but he lacked the motivation to attack it. Instead, he thought of a different motivation. Why should anyone want to abduct Neil Pensom? If it was a practical joke, the hire of a mobile studio and technicians made it a costly and elaborate joke. But if not a joke who would wish to exploit the anxieties of such an inoffensive man? The reference to Marler might be significant.

Samson reread the passage about Marler and then sat back and closed his eyes. It looked as though he was taking a nap but he was concentrating, trying to remember where he had come across the name Marler before. He had a vague recollection that his name had featured in a court case, possibly a case held before licensing justices.

Shandy returned with a glass of hock. After placing it beside the salad she said, 'I've made one enquiry and drawn a blank about GLJ.'

'Keep trying. What's your ploy?'

Shandy raised her voice an octave and said, 'I'm a fifth former on a holiday task. A test of initiative.'

Samson enjoyed listening to the ruses Shandy employed to extract information. A favourite trick, if an interview with a well-known public figure was desired, was to pose as the secretary of a superstar's fan club and say that the superstar was a great admirer of the public figure. Could an interview be arranged for the club magazine? This had worked successfully on a vain politician when Samson had wanted to find out the location of a love-nest. Charmed by Shandy, flattered to be the pin-up of a superstar, the politician had revealed 'strictly off the record' not only the address of the love-nest but had asked Shandy to visit him there that same night.

'Test of initiative,' said Samson. 'How does that go down?'

'Quite well so far. I say we've been set twenty questions which need initiative to find the answer. One of the questions is to find out the name of a television producer or director with the initials GLJ. The switchboard on York-shire TV put me through to a secretary and we had a pleasant little chat but she couldn't help.'

'Who's next on the list?'

30

'Anglia TV.'

'Any reason why you've started with those?'

'Well, from what we know of the teleplay's storyline it focuses on Holland, the North Sea and eastern England. The scenario is less likely to grab, say, Welsh viewers than viewers in eastern regions. And TV companies are very conscious of local interests, apart from the obvious economics. So I'm starting at the east and working west.'

Samson raised his glass of hock to her. 'Good luck.'

On his own once more he picked at the salad. Although he went through a regimen of physical exercise every morning and was fairly fit, he knew his lifestyle, and an appetite for rich food made him at risk from heart attacks. Originally a compulsion to eat had stemmed from loneliness. Eating was a comfort. Now he no longer needed the support of three large meals a day but he had acquired the habit of overeating. For some time Shandy had nagged him to go on a weight-reducing diet and he had finally decided to take her advice.

The salad and hock did nothing to stave off habituated hunger pangs. He pushed the empty plate aside and was about to start reading again when Shandy returned. Her cheeks were slightly flushed, her eyes shining, and she looked what she was, a confident young woman, certain of her place in the scheme of things, and sure of her own ability to cope with anything Fate might throw at her.

'Success,' she said. 'I've found out who GLJ is.'

'Excellent.'

'He's a director with Humberside TV.'

'That's the new station.'

'Right. Someone at Anglia gave me the lead. So I called Humberside. His full name is Geraint Lloyd Jackson. I did the fifth-former act and was put through to his secretary who said he was away for the day and asked if she could help. I went through the ploy and found out he'd directed three well-received serials, all set in the east of England.

31

The last was about disused airfields and a hunt for a man who had an airworthy old Mosquito which he took from airfield to airfield just ahead of the police. He said it was bombed up and was threatening to bomb Buckingham Palace. I remember seeing a couple of instalments. Highly unbelievable but quite gripping.'

'And what's the connection between Jackson and our man?'

'When I asked if a production assistant called Neil Pensom worked with Humberside there was a pause and she said, "I don't recognise the name. . . . Exactly what school are you from?"'

Samson chortled. 'And how did you deal with that?'

'I said I was from Storgate and our art mistress, a Miss Pensom, was always talking about a distant cousin who worked in television. Then the secretary said she was very busy and hung up.'

Samson flicked back through the pages of the typescript. 'Before GLJ had settled on the West Scheldt, "He had been keen on a dike and a polder. Helicopters, and all that."' He looked up. 'That passage refers to the man Pensom is, or was, working for. He is a man who likes aerial photography. I think we may have an interesting case on our hands.' He smiled, showing pink gums and perfect teeth. It was a smile that transformed his heavy features but a certain melancholy seldom left his eyes, and it didn't leave them now.

'I have another little job for you,' he said. 'Try to find out who Marler is.'

Shandy raised her eyebrows. 'Marler?'

'There's a passage in this' – Samson tapped the papers – 'where our client has written about a man called Marler who hates the sight of blood but is utterly ruthless. Our client regrets ever having had any association with Marler. I'd like to know who he is.'

'Oh, great! I could ring around all the Marlers in the

directory and if a man answers ask him if he's utterly ruthless but can't bear the sight of blood.'

'Why not, my dear?'

It was her turn to smile and it was even more attractive than Samson's. 'That's the second time you've called me "My dear", I think I'll put in for a rise.'

'Not granted,' said Samson promptly. 'I've got eleven children to support.'

'The only eleven children you support play football in the Second Division,' she replied, and left the room swinging her hips.

After freshening myself by using water from a container above a tiny wash-basin I returned to the studio and was told that if I gave my word not be awkward, shout, or otherwise attract attention I would be allowed to travel in the back of a car with Beard while a border crossing was made. The car would have a 'Euro' sticker on its windscreen and this would virtually ensure we'd be waved through without having to stop. On the other hand, if I wouldn't promise to be quiet I'd be dumped in the car's trunk and have a very uncomfortable journey.

It didn't take me two seconds to make the decision to say I'd stay quiet. The truck pulled up in a lay-by close to a clump of trees and I was escorted to a waiting Mercedes. When I asked which border we would cross I was told to shut up. And so, with Beard beside me exerting slight pressure on my ribs with his gun, we drove the few kilometres to the border and were, as had been predicted, waved through. It was obvious from road signs that we were now in Germany and for a short distance were on a main road numbered 9 which went to Köln. Soon we pulled off this road and before long were cruising along a minor road which ran between fields of ripe corn.

It was late afternoon and the sky was a vast sheet of peerless blue which deepened in tone towards the east. It

33

was very hot. Sweat beads stood out on Beard's forehead and damp stains showed through the back of the sweat-shirt of our driver, a hatchet-faced man with crew-cut hair.

Beard said that if I guaranteed to behave myself, and not try to make a break for it, we'd get out and stretch our legs. 'Don't forget I've got this,' he said, showing me a snub-nosed revolver.

We got out of the car. It was wonderful to inhale the natural scents of the countryside wafted on a warm, westerly breeze. Beard sneezed. 'Hay fever?' I enquired. sympathetically.

'What if it is? Are you a doctor as well as an agent?'

'No.' I decided to try and pump him. 'Where are we going?'

He shook his head. 'No questions.'

'Can I ask something which has nothing to do with me being here?'

'Go on,' he said guardedly.

'What was the cardgame you were playing? I didn't recognise it and I thought I knew most.'

He looked momentarily disconcerted. Then, 'I don't know its English name. And that's your last question.'

We walked a few paces up and down the road. Two or three cars passed by and I envied the freedom of their occupants. After a few minutes the juggernaut arrived. As it drew to a halt a young couple came into view. They were holding hands and on an afternoon stroll. For a second I thought of yelling, 'Help!' but Beard was menacingly close. I felt the gun poke against my ribs. Obediently mute, I climbed aboard.

Seedy and Medal were seated at the table in the centre of the mini-studio. To the faint but pervasive smell of diesel fuel and the smell of human bodies – it was impossible not to sweat under the bright lights – was added the smell of coffee and I saw that the table was laid with four places and each had a large slice of chicken pie and Russian salad in its place-setting.

34

'Come and join us, Mr Pensom,' said Seedy. 'You must be hungry.'

I wasn't very hungry but thought I should take the opportunity to eat something. I had no idea when the next meal would come.

While we ate Seedy engaged me in polite conversation – Did I like music? Which composers? How about sport? Tennis? – it was all rather unreal. But social niceties were simply a method of wasting time until the meal was finished. Then Medal went to the camera and I realised we were to be filmed again.

Beard left the table and cleared away plates and coffee cups. Out of camera I could see him wolfing the half-finished remains of Medal's slice of pie.

The action began with Seedy enquiring solicitously whether I had enjoyed my supper. 'Not as good as the pies cooked by your wife, I am sure, but quite tasty, I hope.'

'I'm not married. I'm a single man and a television production assistant.'

'No. You are a British agent and you belong to SIS. Your duties are to gather intelligence abroad. We are not sure who is your controller but I think it is the lady who you deny is your wife.'

I said, 'That's crazy.' But it was an understatement. It was outrageous, surreal fantasy.

'Not crazy. Is your wife your controller?'

'I refuse to answer such an absurd question.'

'There is no shame in being controlled by one's wife. Many men are. Domestically and professionally. I will ask the question again. Is she your controller?'

I remained silent.

'You were either given instructions,' said Seedy, 'or you passed on instructions. Which?'

'I don't know what you're talking about.'

'We have removed the film from your camera. There are thirty-four exposures, all of places of interest to diamond merchants.'

'And if I'd had time to reload my camera, which I intended to do in Flushing, you'd have seen a lot of shots of ships, beaches, and anything relevant to the plot we're working on.'

'And this?' Seedy produced a street plan of Antwerp.

'What about it?'

'Is it yours?'

I looked closely. The spot where my hotel, the Eurotel, was situated had a ring inked round it. 'It looks like my map,' I said.

'Yes. It was in your car.' He leaned across the table and a gout of bad breath hit me in the face. 'How do you explain the microdots around the dock area, particularly Straatsburgdok?'

I peered at the map. 'Where?'

'Oh, come now. They aren't still there. They are in process of being enlarged and deciphered.'

I was utterly mystified and said so.

'So you are sticking to your story that you're not an agent of the British government?'

'It's the truth.'

'We shall see. There is some material on videotape. Perhaps you'll change your mind when you've seen yourself on the monitor.'

He said something to Medal who stopped shooting the scene. A cassette was inserted below the monitor. Beard dimmed the lights. And then there was a distraction. The vehicle came to a sudden halt and we were almost thrown sideways. Seedy hurried forward to the driver's cabin. When he returned he said, 'There's an accident ahead. We are in single-line traffic. But that needn't interrupt our show.'

I wished fervently that the truck would have an accident and I could escape. But I was also curious to see what had been filmed and turned my chair to face the monitor.

Beard dimmed the lights further and we were in near

36

darkness. I noticed that Medal had taken up a position just behind me. Did he think I might take advantage of the poor light to start a fight? If so, he was wrong. I am not a coward, but I'm not a lover of this sort of physical contact. And with reason. If I had been I might have chanced my arm long before this.

A colour picture on the screen showed an almost deserted street and a man taking a photograph of the diamond industry showrooms in Hovenierstraat. A zoom-in to close-up showed the man was me. I remembered taking the photograph. It was the last exposure on the cassette.

Next came a couple of shots of me walking down streets as I cut across the city in the direction of Rubens House. The quality of the pictures wasn't very high; it was obvious that a hand-held camera was being used. Up to this point it was an unremarkable film which might have been taken by a tourist. And then came a shot of me waiting for a gap in the traffic before crossing a road and I noticed that four or five people were waiting with me. One of these, standing slightly to my left and behind, was the dreadful Amanda. She reached out and touched, or seemed to touch, my elbow. At the time I'd felt nothing.

The frame was frozen with her hand on my elbow.

'Here we see the first contact,' said Seedy. 'She is making her presence known.'

'I didn't feel anything,' I protested. 'I didn't know she was there. And anyway, she was a complete stranger to me.'

Seedy restarted the tape. As I entered the precincts of Rubens House the woman could be seen walking about twenty paces behind me. Seedy stopped the tape just as I was entering the building.

'We have no record of your discussions,' he said, 'but we do have some stills of you with the woman you call a stranger in the great studio.'

A series of black and white shots followed and they

showed Amanda and me standing in front of Rubens's *Adam and Eve*. A picture of her laughing and me looking as if I'd just cracked a joke. One of us shaking hands. This frame was frozen.

'What were you giving her?' asked Seedy.

'Nothing. We were just shaking hands.'

'Nonsense,' he said sharply. 'Something passed between you. What?'

'Nothing.'

'You are being stupid. We shall find out.'

A shot of me withdrawing my hand from the woman's. A shot of me looking at my watch. A shot of me hurrying away. A shot of her with her hand dipped into her handbag.

'And you still say you gave her nothing,' asked Seedy. 'What then was she putting away?'

'I've no idea.'

Colour flooded the screen again. We were watching a movie once more. There were scenes of open country which could have been part of a travelogue on Holland – a windmill, cows grazing by a canal, three women in traditional costume with lace caps.

'We haven't had enough time to edit this as we would have wished,' Seedy explained.

Then, presumably taken from a camera in a stationary car near the ferry stage, I was seen buying a peach from a fruit-stall. The woman called Amanda moved into camera range and began speaking to me. Then I took a map out of my pocket, had difficulty in unfolding it and she took my peach. The frame of us both looking at the map was frozen.

'That,' said Seedy, 'is obviously a consultation between you which required the use of a map. What were you discussing? Some form of sabotage?'

'Sabotage!' I exclaimed. 'I've never heard anything so ridiculous.'

'No? Then what were you discussing?'

'I was telling her I was on the way to a place called

Vrouwenpolder.'

Seedy giggled. 'And *I* have never heard anything so ridiculous. You had no intention of going anywhere near Vrouwenpolder.'

He was right, of course. I was giving Amanda what is known as a 'bum steer'. I used this expression. It was a bad mistake.

'Bum steer,' he repeated. 'I know bum means the buttocks and a steer is a castrated ox. But how and in what way were you giving her the buttocks of a castrated ox? Was the peach you gave her a symbol of this image?'

'I didn't give her a peach. She took it from me.'

'Husbands and wives often share food. It is a pleasing intimacy.'

I didn't know whether to laugh or cry. I was like an actor in a black farce who doesn't know his lines. 'I was purposely misdirecting her,' I said; 'I wanted to get rid of her.'

'Why?'

'I didn't want her company.' I thought of the mole and the three black hairs. 'I didn't like her looks or the way she was attaching herself to me.'

Seedy gave a supercilious leer. 'You don't expect me to believe that. I'm not a fool. We have a record of you both by the ship's rail.'

The tape continued with the Dutchman coming up and complaining about the ferry's early departure. This frame was frozen. 'Who is he?' Seedy demanded.

'I've no idea. A complete stranger. He was annoyed because the ferry had left ahead of schedule.'

'Stranger,' Seedy scoffed. 'Everyone is a stranger, eh? You call the woman a stranger, now you say the man is a stranger. How is it that you attract so many strangers in one day?'

A sense of frustration swept over me. 'Think what you like. I'd never seen either of them before that day.'

39

The picture on the screen became slightly shaky. A hand-held camera was being used again. A shot of passengers on deck. A small boy crying as a white-haired man scolded him. A family consisting of a very tall man, a slim, fairly tall dark-haired woman, a teenage boy and his younger sister. They were joined by a grey-haired man with a stiff neck. I couldn't imagine why this scene was shot but I could guess what would follow, and I was right. After a view of the estuary of the West Scheldt there followed, at an angle taken from above, a shot of Amanda and me. Although in fact she had been pinning me against the rail it seemed we were in a close embrace. They say the camera cannot lie. But it does. Frequently.

'You are a fast worker,' murmured Seedy, 'if it is true that you'd never met her before that day. I am filled with admiration. I wish you'd teach me the secret of your technique.'

A few seconds later the taped travesty of truth finished. Beard turned up the lights.

'Now then,' said Seedy. 'Let's get down to business. To begin, I want her full name and her position in your organisation.'

'I don't know her full name. She only told me her first name. Amanda. She told me she was exploring Holland and hoping to find her husband. . . .' I began to dry up. It was all so futile. 'That's all I can tell you.'

'There must be a lot more. You were deep in conversation.'

'I wasn't saying anything but platitudes. I was thinking how I could get away from her.'

And then a miraculous intervention occurred. Seedy must have been carrying a bleeper because suddenly it sounded. Bleep. Bleep. Bleep.

He hurried to the radio set and put on headphones, jabbered and then listened attentively. I waited on tenterhooks. Seedy put down the headphones. He rubbed his forehead wearily. A rapid exchange of talk with the other two men followed. It finished abruptly and they were all looking at me. Medal trained the camera on me. Seedy came and sat beside me. 'You are not a British agent,' he announced.

I felt faint with relief.

'We have made a mistake,' he went on. 'I have just heard that the man we want is still in Antwerp. You have the misfortune to resemble him.'

'Thank God you've got it straight at last,' I said, and the faintness cleared. 'I shall expect compensation for the distress you've caused me, including the deprivation of my liberty.'

Seedy considered the matter. After a pause he said, 'You're lucky to be getting out of this alive. We won't dispose of you. We could. Easily. And no one would be any the wiser.'

I felt apprehensive once more. 'What are you going to do?'

Seedy pondered awhile and then, as if he had arrived at the correct decision, said, 'You will be left close to habitation and it will be up to you what to do.'

What he didn't say was that I should be dumped in the middle of the night, trussed like a chicken, in an unknown spot, without passport, papers or anything to identify me. But that's what happened. Eventually the juggernaut stopped. I was blindfolded and led along a path (I assume it was a path because at one point we were in single file) which went up an incline. I was being taken up a hill. At last I heard Seedy say, 'This will do.'

The blindfold was removed but my hands were still securely tied behind my back. The rope was fastened to my ankles so that I was unable to stand. Utterly helpless, and tipped on my side, I was left to face the rest of the night in isolation on the side of a hill. Seedy refused to answer any questions. That is, he refused until he was ready to leave with Beard who had accompanied us. And then, cryptical-ly, he said, 'From here the architect can see his masterpiece on a clear day.'

'What does that mean?' I asked.

'It tells you where you are,' replied a voice out of the darkness. 'But, as a further clue, I'll say I was bluffing when I talked of microdots round the dock area on your plan of Antwerp, but the dock I named was no bluff. Good night. Sleep well.'

Within seconds I was alone, lying on grass, and wondering where the hell I'd been abandoned. Once my eyes were adjusted I saw that against the night sky was a semi-circle of trees behind me and, almost above, a statue loomed. But ahead of me, where the ground sloped down, I could see a distant line of lights and, faintly, I heard the sound of a train.

It was a warm August night and although tied up I was not in great discomfort. My hands could reach the rope where it was knotted above my ankles and gradually I managed to ease the knots. Every so often I paused to avoid cramp. It was during one of these pauses that I noticed the first pale light of day creeping from the east. The statue on a tall stone plinth was black against the skyline. Behind the statue, like a group of acolytes, was a semi-circle of locust trees. It was scenically effective and the artist-technician in me noted it as a suitable location, perhaps as a trysting place for lovers. The fact that I could contemplate professional matters showed my spirits had revived. Admittedly I had no papers of identification, I was tied hand and foot and in a foreign country, but I was alive.

SOME PREDATORS ARE MALE

Part 2

Once my ankles were free I was able to stand upright and exercise stiff leg muscles. The rope round my wrists had become looser and I began picking at knots with my fingers.

The rising sun had by now begun its luminous brush-work and I saw the statue was on the crest of a small hill. A village nestled in the hollow below. To the left, a church spire speared upwards and, to the right, stood a row of poplars and a single factory chimney. The delicate spire and stalk of chimney made a strange juxtaposition but even stranger, and close to where I was standing, was a cemetery. The side of a hill, on the edge of a village, seemed an unusual place for burial and I took a few paces towards it. Every grave was neatly tended and vases of fresh cut flowers were everywhere. Either there had been a local disaster claiming many lives at the same time or the villagers respected their dead, even the long dead. A gardener's shed in one corner of the cemetery probably housed equipment for keeping the place in good order.

For the hundredth time Seedy's cryptic message went through my mind. 'From here the architect can see his masterpiece on a clear day.' And something about the dock in Antwerp not being a bluff. For the life of me I couldn't remember the dock he'd named but it suddenly struck me that the architect might be the person commemorated by the statue. I went to the plinth and saw a lapidary inscription. I can't remember the exact words; the language was German and something was written on all four sides; but it was evidently the statue of Meister Erwin, architect of Strasbourg Cathedral who died in 1318. The statue had been unveiled on 29 August 1844, a date easy to remember as it corresponds with my birthday.

So, on a clear day it might be possible to see Strasbourg Cathedral. I turned to be in line with the same direction as the look on Meister Erwin's rather disdainful face but, although it was a fine day, all I could see was a distant ridge of hills beyond a wide valley. The hills were probably part of the Black Forest. I racked my brains to recall place names but could only think of towns like Bonn and Essen, which would be far to the north. And then, from the right, and coming up a narrow path, a man appeared. He was in a tracksuit and jogging.

I called out. At first he didn't hear me. So I called again and he stopped running and stood close to the gardener's hut. I hurried towards him. I asked if he spoke English. He smiled. 'I hope so. I try to teach it.'

This was a great stroke of luck. Aware that it must sound wildly implausible I explained I'd been the victim of a kidnap but had been released when my captors discovered they had taken the wrong man. I asked him to untie my hands.

He had listened to my account with an air of incredulity, as well he might, but he was quick enough to assist in freeing me.

He told me I was on the edge of a village called Steinbach, about seven kilometres from Baden-Baden. He asked what I was doing in Holland when I was kidnapped and I briefly explained my job.

He thought for a moment. 'Someone will have found your abandoned car. Perhaps there is already a search for you.'

I had already thought about this; it seemed unlikely. If my captors had taken all my papers there would be nothing in the car to identify me. Eventually it would be traced to the hire firm in Antwerp but although they had my Dulwich address there would be no one in the flat to answer any calls. As for GLJ, I couldn't see him panicking and mounting a search unless my disappearance interrupted the shooting schedule, which it wouldn't, as production wasn't due until October.

The German looked me up and down, as if assessing my trustworthiness. I waited hopefully for his verdict. He could either bid me good day and continue jogging or he could offer help.

'My name is Hans Vogel,' he said, extending his hand. 'I think you had better come home with me and we'll contact the police. My wife will give you something to eat. I expect you're hungry.'

'And dirty. I need a wash and shave.'

'That can be arranged. Your name, please?'

I told him.

'Come then, Mr Pensom.'

I followed him down the path and to a gate which opened on to a narrow lane.

We now walked side by side. 'Down there,' he pointed to the left, 'is the pit where clay is excavated. We have a brickworks here which still functions. Over there you see its chimney. Some may say it is a blot on a pretty landscape but it provides employment.'

The lane wound down the hill past small orchards, plots growing garden produce and a vineyard.

'We have a wine co-operative in the village,' he said. 'Next month there will be a festival to mark the fiftieth anniversary of its founding. It will be a big occasion. We have the *Big-Band des Luftwaffenmusikkorps 2* coming from Karlsruhe.'

(Hans, as I came to call him, was later to give me an advance copy of the programme for the four days of the wine festival and it is before me as I write this.)

47

As we passed an unfenced orchard Hans plucked and ate a plum.

'Mmm, good,' he observed. 'Would you like one?'

'No, thanks. . . . Is it your orchard?'

'No. It belongs to an advocate. His wife makes excellent *Pflaumenpastete*, plum tart, delicious with cream. She also makes a very good onion cake. You don't have those in England, I think.'

'No.'

'Her *Gugelhupf* is also out of the world. It is made from an Alsatian recipe.'

I was at a loss what to say. Throughout the walk he behaved like an informative guide or tutor, telling me about the village and its neighbourhood as if deliberately avoiding discussion about my predicament.

As we turned into another lane I saw two or three houses ahead.

'I live there.' He indicated a house which had windows set into a red-tiled roof. Part of the house was screened by trees. 'My wife and I had it built about twenty years ago when we got married.'

He was, as I guessed, only a few years older than me.

'We planted most of the trees,' he went on. 'And the garden produces all the vegetables we need. We have a good crop of tomatoes this year. Do you like tomatoes?'

'Yes, I do.'

'Then you shall have some for your breakfast.'

'Thank you. . . . You said you'd phone the police?'

'Certainly. They'll have to come from Baden. You'll have time for a bath and something to eat.'

'It's very kind of you.'

'Not a bit. The school is on holiday. But if you'd arrived a few days later I wouldn't have been around. My wife and I are taking some senior boys on a trip to your country. We are making a pilgrimage to Stratford-upon-Avon.' He hesitated. 'That is, I shall take the boys there. My wife will

48

probably stay in London. Other arrangements.'

It seemed odd to be talking like this after my experience with the Russians. It was as if I'd been transferred by time-capsule to another world. I found it difficult to orientate myself mentally and although I knew where I was, in a physical sense, it was as if my shadow had become detached and was desperately trying to stitch itself to my heels once more.

We were close to the house. 'Do you like trees?' Hans asked.

'Yes, I do.'

'Do you recognise that one?'

He pointed to a tamarisk-like tree which bore a profusion of red berries.

I said the tree was unfamiliar to me.

'It's a *Sanddorn*. Indigenous to the Rhine region. The berries are rich in vitamin C.'

He spoke like a schoolmaster instructing a pupil on a nature study ramble, and this added to the unreality of my situation.

We mounted some stone steps and Hans inserted a key in the front door. 'Come along in,' he said, standing aside.

I entered a wide hall. Tapestries hung on pinewood walls.

'Gerda,' he called.

A small woman with long black hair, dressed in white blouse and red cotton trousers, came out of an adjoining room. In German too rapid for me to follow Hans explained the position. She looked at me as though I were a stranger from another planet, and this is how I felt. Every time he paused she would say, 'So!' with varying intonations. At last he stopped long enough for her to rattle off a few sentences and from the words I could pick out at random I gathered she was sympathetic. Hans confirmed this. He turned to me.

'My wife says you must be our guest until this matter is

cleared up. She will prepare breakfast for you. I will show you the bathroom and lend you a razor. While you're attending to your toilet, I'll contact the police.'

Twenty minutes later, feeling refreshed and almost of one piece again, I sat down to a meal of cereal, boiled egg, tomatoes and rye bread. A jug of orange juice and a flagon of coffee completed what seemed like a feast.

The house was open-planned. A large L-shaped living room led into a dining annexe. Through open French windows I could see a terrace with garden furniture and beyond this a lawn which sloped upwards towards flower beds and a vegetable garden. Further away, on the side of a hill, were rows of vines. I said something about the pleasing view to Gerda.

Before she could reply Hans appeared from another room. 'Do you say vine-yard or wine-yard?' he asked.

I was to discover he was a man who took his job very seriously and took pains to perfect his English.

'Vine-yard, pronounced "vinyard",' I said.

He nodded. 'Ah, so. Like the old High German *wîngart.*'

Normally I would have been happy to listen to philological comparisons but I was burning to know if he had contacted the police and with what result. He sat down and poured himself a coffee. Gerda fluttered round the table like a small, pretty butterfly. She didn't have an oriental cast of features and yet there was something Japanese about her, traditionally Japanese, that is; passive, attentive and desirous of pleasing her male consort.

Hans took a slice of bread and placed a slice of cheese on it. 'Eat up,' he said, putting action to words. 'The police won't be here yet. Two men are being sent to interview you.' He looked across the table at me. 'I must say they found your story very strange. Indeed they went so far as to suggest it might be a hoax of some sort. A joke. They implied that the *Steinbacher Herbst- und Weinfest* had already started. There is always jollity and good humour at the festival.'

'It's no joke.'

'I know. But you will have to convince them. Have you any proof of who you are?'

'None at all. My passport was stolen.'

'Any proof that you were kidnapped in the Netherlands?'

'No. Only the rope I was tied up with.'

'Ah, yes. The rope. Where is it?'

'We left it by the statue.'

'Perhaps I should go and recover it. It could be proof of some sort, although I can't imagine how.'

'Is the cereal to your taste?' enquired Gerda. 'Some more cream?' Her English wasn't as fluent as Hans's but fairly good.

I assured her it was just right.

'Let us hope,' Hans went on, overriding something Gerda was about to say, 'that your rope isn't a rope of sand. You have that expression in English to mean something apparently strong but worthless when put to the test. We have a similar expression, *schwaches lockeres Band*. We also have a saying equivalent to your "Give a person some rope."'

'Enough rope and he will hang himself,' I said.

'Exactly. But what a strange conclusion to draw. That he should hang himself. Why not, "Give a man enough rope and he will become a ropemaker's salesman and earn himself a big commission"?'

I had no answer to this.

'Have you ever noticed how most popular sayings, both in English and German, date from medieval times and are invariably cautionary or contain predictions of gloom?'

I said I hadn't.

'Our ancestors were intensely superstitious. . . .' And so he went on, quite happy to monopolise the conversation. This suited me well as I am more reticent; more introverted. Gerda sat down close to him, elbows on table, fingers interlaced under chin, and gazed at him as though he were a demi-god.

We finished breakfast and he lighted a cigarette. I was to discover he was something of a chain-smoker. He smoked a brand called *Roth-Händle* which came in a red packet and was manufactured in Baden-Baden. One of the many pieces of useless information Hans imparted was that Dostoevsky probably introduced cigarette smoking to Baden-Baden. He smoked papirossi, a prototype cigarette.

Hans then embarked on a digression about the Russian novel, *The Gambler*, in which the hero (or 'hero-victim' as Hans called him) was modelled on Dostoevsky himself. He had gambled heavily and lost at the Baden-Baden casino. At the time he was having an affair with a young woman called Apollinaria Suslova who teased, tormented and frustrated him. According to Hans, Dostoevsky actually sought out sexual and financial situations which would put him into a high state of anxiety.

While he was giving a lecture on Russian literature (which I imagine he had given a few times in the classroom) I wondered whether I was in some respects similar to Dostoevsky. Not the sexual bit, and certainly not as a literary figure, but more than once I have been excited by anxiety-provoking situations in a financial context.

Hans was lighting another cigarette and talking of Turgenev, who had once lived in Baden-Baden, when the doorbell chimed. The police had arrived.

I had expected men in uniform but both were in well-cut suits that were too warm for the weather. They were sweating slightly and must have been glad of the coolness of Hans's living room.

It wasn't an easy interview. The men were from the detective branch and neither spoke much English. Hans was obliged to act as interpreter some of the time. One of the detectives took down my replies in longhand and this complicated matters as he was keen to get exact meanings and almost all my replies were double-checked for accuracy. He was incapable of grasping that Flushing and

Vlissingen were one and the same place, and I should never have said that I had also wanted to look at Breskens. He got completely muddled. In the end I borrowed his pen and wrote in English, 'Flushing and Vlissingen are one and the same place. Breskens is a town on the opposite side of the river.'

He looked at the statement and in heavily accented English asked, 'But does not Breskens have a second name?'

I could have died with frustration but at last we got away from the tangle of place names. The interview lasted all morning but when I asked which was the nearest British consulate as I would need an emergency document my request was brushed aside.

At one point Gerda served more coffee. Hans opened another packet of cigarettes and the detectives took their ease and discussed with our host the prices of second-hand cars. It seemed that employees of the Mercedes plant were permitted to buy these cars at a discount and frequently sold them at a profit which meant the market price was variable. In a different setting this might have been marginally interesting but I wanted the interview to finish.

'If these gentlemen doubt my story the simplest thing would be to telephone my company.' I gave Hans the number. 'In any event I should very much like to make a call myself. I'll reverse the charges.'

He wrote the number down. 'It isn't that they disbelieve you. It is their wish to be accurate. An example of Teutonic thoroughness,' he added with a laugh.

The interview was resumed. Eventually, when I had told them all I could, even reproducing verbatim conversations with my captors – and by this time Gerda had served glasses of chilled white wine – they stood up simultaneously and both thrust out their hands to be shaken. A flurry of handshakes all round. The detectives shook each other's hands and I found myself shaking hands with Hans as though I too were thanking him for hospitality before leaving.

When the detectives had gone I asked, 'What happens now?'

'You stay here,' said Hans. 'It is not exactly house arrest but I have undertaken that you will not leave until permission is granted. There are two difficulties.'

It seemed there might be more than two, but I queried, 'Two?'

'First, they are unsure whether this is a civil action which you should bring against the alleged kidnappers or a criminal action to be instituted by the State. But, more important, you have committed an offence.'

I was flabbergasted. 'What offence have I committed?'

'Illegal entry,' said Hans. 'You have entered the country illegally. You have not been cleared by the customs authorities. The next step will have to be an interview by officials from customs. They have to decide what, if any, action should be taken against you. Depending on this, the police will be withholding hands in proceedings for the time being.' He frowned. 'Is that correct English?'

'Approximately,' I said wearily. Suddenly I felt desperately tired. Reaction to my ordeal was taking its toll. Or perhaps it was the wine. I would have given anything to lie down on a comfortable bed.

Hans threw back his head and shouted, 'Gerda!'

She came hurrying out from what I guessed was the kitchen.

'We will have a light lunch,' he said. 'Some soup with croûtons, my love. Fruit and cheese to follow.'

'With pleasure,' she said and disappeared.

'May I put through a call to my company?' I asked.

'Ah, yes. I have the number here. I'll get it for you and when there's a connection I'll summon you.'

He was gone less than a minute before returning looking forlorn. 'All lines to England are busy,' he said. 'It is

54

recommended that I call again later in the day.'

He sat down and while we waited for the meal he asked me a number of questions about television, what programmes were popular, the relative importance of different members of the production team, union activity, and so on. I began to feel more relaxed and not so fatigued.

When the soup arrived it was excellent. Described simply as potato soup, it had many ingredients including succulent pieces of smoked bacon. Gerda didn't look like a stereotype *Hausfrau* but she was a magnificent cook.

The telephone rang during dessert. Hans went to answer it. When he returned he said, 'That was the customs people. They can't come until tomorrow. So you will be our guest tonight.'

He looked pleased. I shouldn't have been so pleased if I'd been in his shoes, stuck with a foreigner who was having difficulties with the authorities.

'Gerda will make up a bed for you.'

'It's very kind, but . . .'

'But you cannot leave,' he interrupted. 'So you must stay. You have no alternative. And as you are my guest, my most welcome guest, I suggest the time has come to drop formality. May I call you Neil?'

That is how we came to be on first-name terms.

Gerda, who had eaten frugally and quietly, left the room, came back and said, 'Your room is ready. It is upstairs. I expect Hans will show you the way.'

When he was ready, and after smoking two post-prandial cigarettes, Hans led me upstairs to a room which was where an attic would normally be. It was spacious, light and airy with four large windows set in flush with the roof. Walls and ceiling were panelled with strips of pinewood. Two beds with multicoloured duvets were in the centre of the room which also contained wardrobes, easy chairs, small tables, a scatter of out-of-date fashion magazines, a transistor radio, and a desk beneath one of the windows with a stock of writing paper and a stein filled with coloured pencils and ballpoint pens.

I lay on one of the beds and fell asleep instantly. I came awake to the sound of distant chimes from the church. The clock on the radio showed it was three-thirty in the afternoon. Considerably refreshed, I went to the bathroom which was close to the bedroom and just beyond another small room which might have been a boxroom. I had a shower, cleaned my teeth with a new toothbrush provided by Gerda, and examined my clothes. I needed a change. The shirt had a rim of dirt on the inside of the collar and underpants and socks were weary to say the least.

My mother had always been much concerned with personal hygiene. Towards the end of her life she became quite obsessive about dirt and refused to go on holidays because it would mean having to use strange lavatories and eat from hotel china. I am not nearly so extreme but some of her preferences and prejudices have rubbed off on me and I found the state of my clothes disgusting. I wondered if Hans, who was about my size, would lend me a change while I washed my own clothes. I flatter myself that I can launder and iron as well as any woman and like to think of myself as a self-sufficient man who can look after himself in any sphere of domestic skills – if only I was as adept in financial affairs!

As there was no sound from downstairs I decided to stay in my room for a while. It had occurred to me that it might be a good idea to put on record, for my own benefit, as much as I could remember of the events from the time I hired the car. One advantage of the tedious interview with the detectives was that all sorts of details had been brought to the surface of my mind. Paper and pens were available. I sat down at the desk.

Shortly after five there was a knock on the door and Hans entered.

'Are you rested, Neil?'

'Yes, I'm fine, thanks.'

'I have just tried yet again to make contact with England but the lines are still busy. The exchange is overloaded. Business conventions meeting in Baden seem to have a monopoly of the lines.'

Diffidently I broached the subject of a change of clothes.

'Of course,' he said at once, 'and I won't hear of you washing yours. Gerda will be pleased to do it for you. She has a washing machine which does everything but talk.'

I couldn't help thinking that in Britain Hans would be regarded as a male chauvinist. He seemed to regard his wife as little better than a privileged servant. Strangely she didn't seem to mind; for her it seemed a pleasure to please him.

'It's very kind,' I began.

He held up his hand to stop me. 'It is nothing.' A slightly worried frown creased his forehead. 'Did you hear the telephone shortly after you came up here?'

'No. I fell asleep at once.'

'It was the police. They cannot find the rope. They searched everywhere around the statue of Meister Erwin.'

'Someone must have found it and taken it for himself.'

'Exactly what I said, but they weren't satisfied. They like to have evidence, even circumstantial evidence.'

'But you saw I was tied up,' I exclaimed.

'Most certainly. And I will depose – if that's the correct word – if necessary.' The frown disappeared. 'Would you like to come down for a cup of tea? I know the English like their tea in the afternoon.'

Together we went downstairs.

Gerda was in the living room arranging a vase of flowers. She was wearing a white cotton dress with a scarlet sash round the waist. Her bare arms and legs were brown and she looked very pretty. If I were the sort of man easily aroused by female beauty she could have aroused me. As it was, I admired her as one might admire a delicate work of art. She looked at me over the purple bloom of an aster. 'Are you well rested, Mr Pensom?'

'Very well, thank you.'

'I am glad.' She continued to arrange flowers.

'Gerda, my love,' said Hans brusquely, 'will you get us some tea? I will then let our friend have a change of clothing and perhaps you would wash what he is wearing now.'

I felt embarrassed by this peremptory demand but before I could say anything she had replied, 'With pleasure. Yes, I will make some tea. Milk or lemon, Mr Pensom?'

'Milk, please.'

She glided away with the lissom grace of a Japanese geisha.

I told Hans I must contact a British consulate. This was necessary if a UK passport was lost or stolen.

'Of course,' he said. 'We will do it after tea.'

'Where is the nearest consulate?'

'I don't know. Freiburg maybe. We'll find out. But your consulate won't be able to help until police enquiries are completed and you've been cleared by customs. I know that for a fact. Last year a teacher on an exchange visit to Baden lost his passport and his consulate couldn't do anything until police enquiries had been completed, and this was a simple loss, not a theft.' He slapped my shoulder in a friendly manner. 'Don't worry. You'll be all right here. *Ein Mann, ein Wort! Ehrlich!* What's your expression – word of honour?' With a smooth verbal gear change he switched from consulates to universal clichés.

It was boring, but I had to listen. After all, I needed to keep his goodwill.

Gerda joined us for tea and listened attentively to her husband's monologues although I guessed she must have heard them a thousand times before. She even laughed, a musical laugh, at a stale joke about the Berlin wall.

Eventually he ran out of steam and we went to his dressing room, a small room attached to the principal

58

bedroom. He selected a candy-striped shirt in red and light grey, charcoal grey slacks and a black leather jacket. The ensemble looked quite well on me although these weren't colours I would have chosen.

Hans left me on my own to change and while I was trying on the jacket I heard the telephone ringing. A minute later he came hurrying in. 'Good news, my friend. That was a call from the police. Your passport has been found together with some other papers.'

'Thank heavens for that.'

'Thank heavens indeed. They will bring it tomorrow.'

'Where was it?'

'A woman found it in a plastic bag lying in the gutter somewhere near Trier. It must have been thrown out of the truck.' He stood back and appraised my new outfit. 'It looks better on you than it does on me,' he said enthusiastically. 'Come, let us show Gerda.'

She wasn't so enthusiastic and I had the impression she didn't care to see another man wearing her hero's apparel.

It was while I was rather foolishly parading around the living room being directed this way and that by Hans as he tried to whip up a more positive response from his wife that we heard the musical chimes of the front door bell. Glad to be released from the conflict of praising something she didn't wish to praise, but fearing no praise might displease, Gerda hurried away.

She came back looking bewildered, wide-eyed and shaking her head. She said something in German to Hans. He jerked as though an electric current had been passed through him. Turning to me he said, 'I thought you told me you weren't married.'

'I'm not.'

'Then what is your wife doing at my front door?'

The hurt and indignation in his voice hardly pierced the shock I felt at this grotesque absurdity. I have no wife; I have never wanted to have a wife and, if I have any say in

59

the matter, I never shall have a wife. The idea of matrimony, of being legally bound to one person of the opposite sex, is my idea of direst punishment.

'What is your wife doing at my front door?' Hans repeated.

Gerda's eyes were saucers of recrimination. If I had slaughtered a baby in front of her she couldn't have looked more accusatory.

'This is a nonsense,' I managed to say. But it was more than a nonsense. It was a ghastly repeat of the accusations made by Seedy.

'How did she find you here?' Hans asked. 'How? How? Your business is your business, but how?'

I collected my wits. 'There's obviously been a mistake,' I said. 'Where is this imposter?'

As if on cue, she entered. She walked in. It was Amanda.

'Darling,' she said.

I recoiled. I could see her advancing with the light of an embrace in her eyes. The hairs on her mole were rigid with determination.

I said something stupid, something I was to regret. I said, 'How did you find me?'

What I meant was, 'When I last saw you was when I gave you the slip at Flushing and saw your car heading in the rough direction of Vrouwenpolder, so how did you come to trace me here, and why are you pretending to be my wife when you know very well we met for the first time yesterday morning in Rubens House?' That is what I meant. But to Hans and Gerda 'How did you find me?' sounded like the cry of an errant husband confronted by a wifely Nemesis.

She advanced, arms outstretched. I retreated behind a table.

Hans spoke. He said, 'I think we should leave these two people alone to patch up their differences, my love.'

Gerda nodded in agreement.

'Don't go,' I pleaded. 'This isn't true. I'm not married to her. I don't know what's happening but I'm being set up.'

'Set up,' said Hans, his intellectual curiosity aroused, 'I haven't heard that expression. Is it the opposite of "Sit down"?'

'It means that for some reason someone is trying to fix me, to put me in a false position.'

'You are ill, darling,' said Amanda from the other side of the table. 'I'll look after you. Nurse you. You want to know how I found you? Well, when you went astray at Triberg I reported to the chief of police. He contacted all divisions and from Baden-Baden came news that you were at a house in this village.' She looked me up and down approvingly. 'I like you in that jacket. It suits you.'

I had never before heard of Triberg.

'You can't believe this rubbish,' I said to Hans. 'You found me tied up by the statue. And the police have found my passport in Trier.'

'That's right,' said Amanda. 'They did. What were you doing in Trier, you naughty boy?' She turned to Hans. 'Tied up, was he? He has this eccentricity.'

Hans gave me a slyly curious look. 'Ropes, eh? I have often thought the Reeperbahn in Hamburg, with its catering for fantasies, well named.' In case I didn't understand the allusion, he explained, 'Reeperbahn is German for rope-walk.'

If I had been a child I would have screamed, 'I want to go home! Let me go home!' But I am an adult and have to adopt adult stances and logic.

Coldly I said, 'The first time in my life I ever saw this woman was yesterday in Antwerp. She was a nuisance then, and she's a nuisance now. I don't know what her game is or why I've been picked on for this ridiculous charade but I swear I've told you the truth.' I paused, and for added emphasis said again, 'I never set eyes on her before yesterday.'

61

'Set eyes,' murmured Hans. 'I really must acquaint myself better with the verb "to set". First, it's set up; now it's set eyes. A truly versatile verb.'

For once Gerda was tough with her hero. 'Stop talking like a schoolmaster,' she said sharply. 'This is serious. Our guest has run away from his wife and we have them both in our house. What are you going to do?'

We all looked at Hans and waited for his answer. 'I think the best thing,' he said, 'is to leave them alone to patch up their differences.'

'She is not my wife,' I said firmly. 'She is an imposter.'

'*Kein Rauch ohne Feuer*,' observed Gerda.

My German was adequate enough to translate, 'There's no smoke without fire.' So she actually believed there was some truth in the ghastly Amanda's allegation. And so did Hans. He gave me a sad smile and said, 'I think, my friend, you are learning the great truth expressed by the poet Schiller. *Der Wahn ist kurz, die Rau'ist lang.* The illusion of love is brief, the repentance long.' Taking his wife by one of her slender brown arms he piloted her out of the room. At the doorway he called out, 'You are both our guests until this matter is disposed of.'

Alone with Amanda I said, 'What's the game?'

She smiled and a shark's smile would have been more winsome. 'There is no game, darling. Have you forgotten everything?'

'Such as?'

'Such as our wedding at the registry office in Sevenoaks. Or our honeymoon in Majorca when you ate too much fruit and got the runs. You said it was nerves but I knew it was the fruit.'

The sheer mendacity of this preposterous lie took my breath away. She was round the table while I was gasping and off-guard. 'Don't worry,' she said, grasping my arm, 'everything will be all right. Amanda will look after you.'

I wrested my arm away and managed to put the table

between us once more. 'I don't know what you're playing at, or how you found me here, but even if there was any truth in this farrago of nonsense there'd be no question of you looking after me, here or anywhere else.'

'Come home with me. Back to England.'

'Even if I wanted to, which I most positively don't, I can't go anywhere. I'm under house arrest.'

Her hand flew to her mouth in alarm. 'What have you been doing? You haven't been a naughty boy, have you?'

I looked longingly at the open French windows. I could escape up the vineyard, but then what? I had no passport.

'Have you been a naughty boy, Neil? You can tell me. I understand your funny little ways.'

Although I am inhibited from being rude to women I said, quite viciously, 'Get lost.'

She clucked like a hen. 'You are in a bad way. Get lost? You are the one who's lost. Selective amnesia Doctor Toogood called it. Don't you remember?'

If one is a selective amnesiac, does one remember the selective amnesia or is lack of such memory part of the selective amnesia? The thought flitted through my mind before I could put a caustically rhetorical question. She was saying, 'Why can't you come home? What have you been doing?'

I parried question with a question. 'How did you find me?'

'What have you been doing?'

'How did you find me?'

'What have you been doing?'

'How did you find me?'

In chess terms it was perpetual check.

She broke the deadlock. 'I've told you. Have you forgotten already? It was through the good offices of the chief of police in Triberg.'

'I've never been to Triberg. I never met you before Antwerp. You're trying to fix me, or you're working for someone who's trying to fix me. Who? Why?'

She wrung her hands in a gesture of despair. It occurred to me she might be an actress hired to play a part. I took a chance. I leaned across the table to peer at her and said, 'Now I think of it, I have seen you before. It was on the stage. Where was it? Huddersfield? Ipswich? Or did you play in the West End?' This last was more subtle than it may seem. I've never met a minor actor or actress who doesn't regard it as prestigious to have played London's West End and will let it drop that they've appeared at Wyndhams, the Criterion, or whatever.

But she was sufficiently good an actress not to be thrown. Perhaps she wasn't a professional actress, after all. Unperturbed by my bait she said, 'What did you mean when you said you were under house arrest?'

It wasn't her business but I decided to tell her precisely what had happened since we parted ways in Flushing. When I'd finished she said, 'I'm not sure selective amnesia was the right diagnosis. Not unless you add pathological lying to it.'

In such circumstances the human instinct is either to fight or flee. I could do neither. I was a fly stuck to a web and she was a ravenous spider.

We had been facing each other over a table but suddenly she turned and went to a chair and sat down. 'Here I am,' she said, 'and here I stay.'

I couldn't see Hans accepting this and my spirits rose. 'The owner of this house might have something to say about that.'

'Let's ask him.'

'Yes, let's.'

'Herr Vogel,' she shrilled.

A moment later Hans came in. 'You called?'

'*Ja, Ich möchte ein Zimmer* . . .' Off she went in a stream of fluent German which left me stranded. How I wished I had studied German more seriously at school, but Mother was a

Francophile and in her autocratic way discouraged any attempts to learn anything foreign but French culture and language.

The rapid exchange between Hans and Amanda terminated abruptly when she unfastened her handbag and produced a wad of banknotes. To my horror Hans accepted them. He was selling my freedom to this termagant.

He turned to me, eyes downcast like any traitor's. 'I have arranged with your wife that she shall stay here until the authorities give you permission to leave.'

'She is *not* my wife.'

'No. I understand the problem. She has explained it. You must not distress yourself. It doesn't help your condition.' He lifted his eyes. 'In fact, argument makes it worse. Your wife will be my guest here.'

'Then I'm leaving.'

'I beg you not to think of doing anything so foolish. If you do' – he paused to give emphasis to what followed – 'I shall be obliged to inform the authorities at once. You would be arrested as an illegal immigrant and thrown into jail.'

'I should demand to see the British consul.'

He gave me the sorrowful but stern look of a schoolmaster about to deal with a fractious child. 'That would do you no good at all. You have nothing to show to prove you are British, not even your clothes. They would laugh at your demands.'

'She's bribed you!'

'Not bribed. I have been paid for providing accommodation.' He wagged a finger at me. 'Don't forget, you were welcome here without charge.'

'Thank you very much,' I said bitterly.

My sarcasm was wasted; he thought I was genuinely grateful. 'That's better,' he smiled. 'Now then, we are rather short of accommodation. The other spare room is being decorated. You and your wife will share a room tonight.'

'I refuse.'

'There are twin beds.'

'I refuse. I'd sooner go to jail.'

'Very well, that can be organised,' he said ominously. 'But I warn you, it would greatly delay your departure from our country. It will certainly mean you'll be formally charged with illegal entry, otherwise there would be no justification to imprison you with the consequent charge upon taxpayers.'

I was beaten.

'I can sleep down here,' I said. 'On the floor, if necessary.'

'No,' he replied sharply. 'I will not allow it. In my house you do as I say. You will share a bedroom with your wife.'

Amanda was smiling triumphantly.

'When I get to the bottom of this,' I fumed, 'someone is going to pay, and pay dearly.'

'Yes, yes, of course. Pay dearly.'

'Don't bloody well humour me!'

'I wouldn't dream of it.'

A silence fell. Rather nervously Gerda entered the room. I guessed she'd been listening outside the door.

Most of the rest of the day passed in a haze. Amanda and the Vogels chatted away in German like old friends occasionally throwing me crumbs of English about the weather or the political situation. Every so often Amanda would say, 'How are you feeling, darling?'

There's nothing more irritating than solicitous enquiries based on false premises, pursued with remorseless disregard of truth. I began to realise what it must feel like to be wrongly committed to a mental institution.

The evening meal was beautifully prepared and cooked and I was glad of that because Amanda stuffed herself, and eating kept her reasonably quiet. Hans, to give him credit, although I hadn't yet forgiven him for accepting a bribe to back Amanda against me, treated me like a normal human being. As he had earlier in the day, he asked questions about my job and was obviously fascinated by television. I was happy to satisfy his curiosity. In fact, I think it kept me from going mad with frustration. Needless to say, he hadn't managed to get a line to England until quite late and then there was a permanently engaged signal. In the end I gave up. After all, tomorrow I should get my passport back and then, providing the customs or immigration officials weren't awkward – I wasn't clear which branch was involved; Hans sometimes spoke of one and sometimes of the other – I'd be winging my way home and away from this nightmare.

Hans was generous with wine and I drank heavily to dull my senses. Strangely the alcohol had little effect and my faculties weren't blurred when Hans announced it was time for bed. I made a last desperate attempt to avoid a fate almost worse than death but nothing would deter my self-appointed 'wife' from sharing my room, and Hans was adamant that I couldn't sleep elsewhere.

Amanda went to her car and brought a holdall indoors. It contained a pink nightdress. She called it shocking pink. It was ghastly pink. She held it up in front of her ample body for Gerda, Hans and me to admire. *'Sehr schön,'* said Gerda. *'Ja, sehr schön,'* said Hans. Amanda turned towards me, eyebrows raised in enquiry.

I couldn't risk alienating her too much if I was to spend the night in her company. On the other hand I didn't want to give the slightest encouragement. I steered a middle course. 'Very shocking,' I said.

She led the way upstairs. I followed, my eyes level with her posterior which waggled quite dizzily. I stayed in the bathroom while she undressed.

'Ready,' she called.

An aristocrat on the threshold of the guillotine couldn't have felt more apprehensive than I did at the sound of that gleefully carolled 'Ready'.

I dragged myself into the bedroom. 'What do you really think of it?' she asked, and began to parade around in the shocking-pink creation. 'Do you like it?'

'It's certainly pink. No one could say it isn't pink.'

'Does it remind you of our honeymoon?'

I said, 'This has gone far enough,' and even as I spoke I knew I had uttered one of the stalest of all clichés.

She beamed at me and the hairs on her mole semaphored a warning of hideous delights. With unexpected agility she seized a pillow. 'Let's have a fight, darling.'

'Let's not. Let's be sensible.'

'Who wants to be sensible when love is in the air?'

I retreated behind the bed I regarded as my bed as I'd slept on it that afternoon.

'Come on,' she said, and she threw the pillow at me. I fielded it with dexterity and she grabbed another pillow. 'Now we're both armed,' she said. 'Have at you, knave!'

A ridiculous chase ensued. Medusa flailed with her pillow and I dodged with footwork that wouldn't have disgraced a bantam-weight boxer.

At last fitness told. I was the more fit. She collapsed on her bed, exhausted. 'Why won't you play?' she asked in an aggrieved voice. 'You used to like it.'

'I don't know what this is all about,' I said, 'but I intend to find out, and I shall sue you for every penny I can get.'

She leered at me. 'On what grounds? Not non-consummation of marriage surely?'

I was bereft of speech and she laughed at me. 'Never mind, Mummy knows how to look after naughty boys.'

How dared she say a thing like that! It was an insult to my mother. Momentarily I lost control. 'You bitch,' I snarled.

She laughed again. 'Naughty, naughty.'

She sat on the side of her bed and, to my intense relief, put down her pillow. 'All right,' she said. 'Come and give Amanda a good-night kiss.'

68

Until that moment my greatest dread would have been to have been keelhauled by pirates on the Spanish Main as I have a morbid fear of deep water, but Amanda's invitation eclipsed that dread.

I managed to say, and with some dignity I hope, 'There will be no kissing. Good night.'

She was still panting from her exertions and I guessed she wouldn't start another pillow fight. I climbed into bed, slid under the duvet and switched off the bedside lamp.

'Why did you do that?' she demanded. 'You know I can't sleep unless all the lights are on.'

I didn't move. The overhead light and her bedside lamp were still on.

'Very well,' she said, 'but I shan't forgive you.'

A few moments later I heard the groan of springs as she settled into bed.

Silence. Time passed. I couldn't relax. Every muscle, every nerve, every sinew, was screwed up to maximum tension. It was only when I heard regular deep breathing that I began to relax. But I couldn't sleep. I am not able to sleep with the lights on. Eventually, after weighing the pros and cons, I crept out of bed and switched off all the lights. She didn't stir. At last, it must have been past three in the morning, I fell asleep.

I woke first and crept past the sleeping beauty to the bathroom. After shaving and dressing I tiptoed out of the bathroom and slunk downstairs. Hans was already in the living room.

'Did you sleep well?' he asked.

For the first time we were alone together. No Amanda, no Gerda. I pleaded, I begged, I insisted he accept my story as the truth. I had never seen Amanda before meeting her by chance in Antwerp. She was not my wife. Someone – I didn't know who – was playing a wicked practical joke on me.

He listened politely. In the end he said, 'English humour

is a mystery to all Europe. I will accept this is a joke. But I am afraid that you must also accept that under German national law you cannot leave until immigration have cleared your entry and you have your passport. That being so will you please play along with the madness of this joke.'

I asked what he meant.

'I mean you should pretend you are married. If you do, things will be very much easier. Allow your wife – forgive me, your so-called wife – to have her way. Pretend you entered quite legally and ran away from her at Triberg. Your story of kidnap was a foolish lie, even a hallucination, and you are very sorry for causing so much trouble. The customs will no doubt be lenient and the police will return your passport. Indeed, if you were to make out it was all caused by some domestic dispute they'll be only too glad to clear off. Officials never like to get involved in such matters. But if you don't play it the way I'm suggesting, and you insist on your version of events, there could be complications.'

He spoke with such conviction I was in two minds what to do for the best.

'Come now,' he said, 'you can pretend for a little while. Once you have your passport and the customs are satisfied that because of your mental state there is no point in pursuing the matter, you will be free. You can then give her the escape. No, that's not correct. Give her . . .'

'The slip?'

'That's it. Give her the slip.'

Silence fell between us as I considered the idea.

'It's another lovely morning,' said Hans. 'It would be nice to be free.'

I looked through the French windows. A thrush was perched on the branch of an apple tree. Above the summit of the vine-covered hill the sky was pure blue. Two cheeping sparrows flew past.

'You found me,' I said. 'You know I was tied up.'

'Only your hands were tied and you could have tied them yourself. You were practically free.'

'You don't think . . .'

'I believe you,' he interrupted. 'I am simply telling you it is better sometimes to bend the truth in the cause of self-interest. Sacred self-interest.'

I don't know whether it was this euphemism for lying which persuaded me but I began to see the force of his argument. Our eyes met and there was a twinkle in his. 'Bend the truth in the sacred cause of self-interest,' he repeated and the corners of his mouth twitched in amusement.

In all relationships except the most static there are moments when you feel a step has been taken towards or away from deeper understanding. This was such a moment.

'Bend the truth in the sacred cause of self-interest,' I solemnly affirmed.

'*Ja*, that is right!'

We both laughed. It was as if a pact had been sealed.

I felt almost cheerful. A burden was beginning to lift. I would play Amanda's mad game until I'd got my passport and then I'd be free as the birds in the garden.

Gerda came down in a pretty floral housecoat, her lustrous hair piled high on her head, and she glided quietly about laying the breakfast table while Hans embarked on a polemic about the SPD, a political party.

The table had been laid and an appetising aroma of coffee was wafting in from the kitchen before Amanda appeared.

'Why didn't you wait for me?' she demanded accusingly.

Hans gave me a look which had the effect of a starter's gun. I sprang from my blocks. 'I'm sorry, darling,' I said, 'I thought you would prefer to sleep on.'

Her eyes narrowed. It was an are-you-having-me-on look and for the first time I knew I had the advantage.

Gerda materialised. 'Did you sleep well?' she asked

Amanda in English.

'Well enough. But my husband isn't the man he was. On our honeymoon it was very different.'

'Yes?' enquired Gerda encouragingly.

Hans could see I was irked by her lying implication and gave a cautioning glance. I restrained myself. At least her lie was preferable to a pretence that we'd made love all night long.

'He used to be very romantic,' she said to Gerda. And, to me. 'Remember, darling?'

I willed myself to sound enthusiastic. 'How could I forget? The happiest days of my life.'

This was going over the top and I received a look of such sharp severity I almost lifted my arms to fend off a slicing blow.

'I hope you are not trying to be funny, my love.'

'Far from it,' I replied boldly. 'Wonderful days.'

'But very different now. You haven't kissed me good morning yet.'

I steeled myself, leapt from my seat and went to dab a kiss on her cheek. But in the split-second pause while I aimed to avoid her mole with its wiry antennae she turned her face and kissed me on the lips. Her lips were soft and the kiss not unpleasant. It was a bit disturbing.

'That's better,' she said. 'I'm glad to see you're back to normal and there's no more silly talk about being kidnapped.'

'No. I was foolish to run away at Trier.'

'It was Triberg. Trier was where they found your passport.'

'Of course.' I slapped my brow, the stage action of someone chastising a flagging memory. 'I was foolish to run away at Triberg.'

'Good. I am glad to hear you say it. And after these kind people have given us breakfast we will continue our tour.'

'Yes, I'm looking forward to it.'

How I managed to sustain this demeaning charade I shall never know, but fortunately Gerda was ready with lightly boiled eggs, and breakfast began. Hans who had given silent encouragement with winks and nods now took over the conversation and gave me a breather. This time it was a string of school anecdotes, few of which I remember, but all of which culminated in hearty laughter from Hans, guffaws from Amanda, a pretty laugh from Gerda (who had evidently heard all the stories before but as a supportive wife concealed boredom) and laughs from me which were basically expressions of goodwill towards Hans.

It was as breakfast was finishing that two officials from the immigration department called. Like their police counterparts they were in plain clothes. They interviewed me in the living room for about twenty minutes. I improvised brilliantly, interspersing the fiction with apologies for causing inconvenience.

My story of abduction was false. I had come from England in the company of my wife for the purpose of a tour. We had hired a car and entered Germany quite legally. Satisfied by this fairy tale they left. Minutes later the police arrived. They didn't even ask to see me. Hans went to the front door and when he returned he was holding a plastic bag triumphantly aloft.

I sent a jug of cream flying in my haste to leave the table. My precipitate dash to grab the bag was because I was afraid Amanda might intercept, claim the bag for herself, and keep the passport as a hostage for my future good behaviour.

'Clumsy!' shouted Amanda. 'Look what you've done. Get him a cloth, my dear Frau Vogel. He shall clean it up.'

I didn't care. I'd got my passport. I mopped up the floor while Amanda stood over me like some Amazonian slave-driver. The humiliation of the situation didn't hit me until later. When the cream was mopped up, and there wasn't much, the two women cleared the table and went to stack dishes in the dish-washer.

While they were in the kitchen Hans whispered, 'Now is your chance. I've left the front door open.'

He thrust a bunch of fifty-mark notes into my hand.

'How can I ever repay. . .'

'No need. This is the money she gave me. *Geh' endlich.* Go! Go!'

A quick handshake and, I am not ashamed to say, I fled through the front door like an escaping cage-bird. In the blindness of jubilation I almost crashed into a car parked much too close to the house. As I recovered my balance I recognised the car. It was the one which Amanda had driven on to the ferry at Breskens. My mind operated in overdrive. Could I immobilise it? It would take too long to remove the distributor head. And then I noticed the ignition keys had been left in their socket. I was about to reach inside and take them when my racing mind clicked into an even more supercharged groove. I wouldn't take the keys; I would steal the car!

Hardly believing my luck I climbed in. The engine fired almost at once. I slammed the gears into reverse, backed out grazing a wall in the process, got into first and was on my way, roaring down a narrow road into the village proper. Avoiding a head-on collision with another car by a fraction I realised I was driving on the wrong side of the road. Collect your wits, Pensom, I said to myself.

Soon I reached a main road. A sign pointed in the direction of Baden-Baden. To me it was a heavenly sign, a divine finger pointing to freedom. I turned to follow its direction and was soon speeding away from the village eternally renowned as the birthplace of Meister Erwin.

SOME PREDATORS ARE MALE

Part 3

Samson put down the typescript. After a few moments' thought he went to the window. Often when he felt like a break from desk work he would idly gaze out at the busy street scene below. But today he looked at the building opposite which, by a first floor window, had a sign advertising office premises, with flat above, to let on a long lease.

For some time he had been thinking about a move. His own flat was about a mile from the office and in a Victorian tenement house which had a facade blotched by peeling stucco. The tenements on either side were boarded up and occupied by squatters. The street was part of an area of urban decay which rain never refreshed and sunlight could not brighten. The view from Samson's front window was of a row of ageing buildings including a Methodist church, two boarded-up shops and a newsagents. It was a depressed and depressing part of south London but it wasn't the melancholy and sordid environment that Samson objected to; it was the amount of time it took him to travel from home to office.

Sometimes he used public transport, sometimes he hired a car and sometimes he went on foot, but the journey was always tedious, and pedestrian and road traffic heavy. He had made up his mind either to move right away from the office or to move as close as possible. But the purchase price of the premises opposite was unrealistically high. He had made an offer which had been rejected and now he was waiting to see if the vendors would either sell to someone else or bring down the asking price.

His thoughts switched to what he had been reading. There was something too literary, too contrived, too self-consciously constructed about Pensom's account of his misadventures. Some people possessed total recall and had an eidetic memory but this faculty was extremely rare. And, even if one accepted that the dialogue was accurate, how could a professed ignorance of German language square with the fact that expressions in German were quoted, including a quotation from Schiller? Either Pensom wasn't telling the truth when he disclaimed knowledge of German or someone else had helped him write the story, even ghosted it.

But, the writing style apart, there were a number of suspect points. It seemed unlikely, if German bureaucracy was anything like the British, that Amanda would have traced her 'husband' so quickly. And it wasn't clear whether the customs or the immigration department were concerned about illegal entry. For someone so accurate on other matters this seemed vague. And he seemed to regard Amanda as merely an instrument in a monstrous joke, not its initiator. Why not? And was it a joke or something more sinister?

But the one inconsistency that remained in Samson's thoughts and kept recurring like a nagging ache was that Hans Vogel was a jogger. People jogged to keep fit. They were fanatical about their health. And yet Vogel was a chain-smoker. Jogging and chain-smoking didn't tally; the one excluded the other.

Samson returned to his desk and resumed reading.

Baden-Baden is a beautiful town with fine buildings, well-tended gardens and an atmosphere not too ostentatiously up-market. Or so Hans had told me. But to me Baden-Baden was a confusing place with too many one-way streets. Hans had also said that like Heidelberg it had emerged unscathed from World War II and the city council were determined to maintain its quiet charm and character. They had even made the ubiquitous Macdonalds fast-food restaurant conform to the environment.

Hans had told me that no one should visit the town without paying a visit to the Kurhaus. In different circumstances I wouldn't have missed playing at the casino where Dostoevsky had gambled but this time I couldn't follow Hans's recommendation. The theft of Amanda's car would be reported and I wanted to abandon it as soon as possible, but I also needed to get to the railway station. I imagined this station would be somewhere near the centre of town. I was wrong. It is on the perimeter and incredibly difficult to find if one's German is inadequate. I drove round in circles and became frantic as, trapped by one-way systems, I kept returning to the centre. I was like a low-calibre rat stuck in a maze easily learned by first-year rats. If it had happened to Kafka he would have transmuted the experience to an epic of frustration. But at last, on the verge of despair, I found the station having been told by a helpful English-speaking pedestrian that the signs 'Bahnhof' were the ones to follow.

Stuttgart was the nearest German airport but there was no direct connection between Baden-Baden and Stuttgart for at least four hours. So I took the train to Karlsruhe and changed there. When finally I arrived at the airport it was difficult to book a flight but eventually I boarded a Lufthansa 737 bound for Heathrow.

The flight was uneventful but it made me smile wryly when the captain announced over the intercom that we were just north of Trier and would pass by Liege, Brussels and Ostend. Just north of Trier. The place where my passport was found. I felt in my pocket to make sure it hadn't gone homing like a pigeon back to Trier.

It was a wonderful feeling when the wheels touched the

runway and there was a whoosh of reverse thrust as the pilot braked. I had nothing to declare at customs and went straight to an exchange bureau to convert marks into pounds sterling. I hired a taxi and within an hour was at my apartment block.

My keys had never left me, unlike my passport, and so there should have been no problem. The first key was for opening the entrance door to the apartments, the second key was for opening my flat. The first key worked but to my astonishment the second key didn't fit. What had gone wrong? I twisted and turned but nothing happened. Suddenly the door opened and a woman I didn't recognise said, 'What the hell is going on? What are you trying to do?'

I had already checked the number but I checked again. 'This is number fourteen,' I said. 'My flat. Who are you?'

'Your flat! Are you a weirdo?'

I must have looked at her aghast. I felt aghast. What was this woman, who looked like a starlet, rippling blonde hair and pouting lips, dressed in diaphanous nonsense which revealed nipples big as the studs on a footballer's boots, doing in my flat?

'This is my flat,' I said. 'What are you doing here?'

'Your flat? You must be joking.'

I told her emphatically that I wasn't joking and, for good measure, said I would have to call the police.

She smiled sensuously. 'Go ahead. Would you like to use my phone? Come on in.'

Her invitation poleaxed me. I was being invited into my own flat by an intruder to make a telephone call which could only result in her eviction. I was so shaken I checked yet again I was at the right flat. All floors of the block are similar in design; perhaps I was on the floor above or below my own flat.

'Which floor am I on?' I asked the woman who was posing against the door, draping herself against oak veneer and caressing the brass keyhole with long fingers tipped with blood-red nails. She was in no hurry to answer me. I repeated the question.

She looked down at polished parquet. 'You're standing on it,' she said, and laughed.

I contained annoyance. 'Is this the third floor?'

She nodded.

'Then it's my floor and this is my flat. Number fourteen.'

The nodding changed to a slow head-shake. 'No, sir. It's my flat but you're welcome to make your phone call. Come in and have a drink. I could use a bit of company.'

Welcome or not, I was determined to enter. The flat contained all possessions dear to me including mother's collection of silver spoons which I'd promised never, on any account, to sell. The woman stood back as I walked purposefully past her into the small hall.

Something was wrong, and when I entered the living room I almost passed out with shock. My flat had been completely refurnished, not a single piece of furniture was mine.

I swayed on my feet and she assisted me to a chair. 'Sit down. You look all in. Can I get you a brandy?'

'Who are you?' I managed to say.

I hardly heard her reply because I'd noticed with immense relief that the carpet hadn't been changed, and nor had the wallpaper. This was my flat. I hadn't gone mad.

'Sorry,' I said. 'I missed that. Who did you say you were?'

This time I made the effort to impress her words on my memory.

'My name is Felicity Flowerdew. I'm a model. I have no regular boyfriend. I like to travel and I swim whenever I can.'

She looked and sounded like a competitor in a Miss World contest.

'Felicity?'

81

'Flowerdew.'

'What are you doing in my flat and where has all my stuff gone?'

I attempted to stand but was slightly off balance and she pushed me back on to the chair with remarkable strength. 'You relax. I'll fix you a drink. Brandy OK, or would you prefer Scotch?'

'Brandy.'

She disappeared into the kitchen and I took the opportunity to nip across to the window. Although I knew this was my flat I was still slightly disorientated and wanted to double-check by seeing the view outside.

By now it was late afternoon and the sun was shining full on the next block. Its rays striking a pane of glass made a dazzling square of light. I looked down on an ornamental garden with a lily pond in its centre. The scene was exactly as it should be. I went back to my chair just as Felicity Flowerdew came in carrying two glasses.

'It's a bit early,' she said, 'but I think I'll join you.' She handed me a balloon-glass of brandy. 'Cheers,' she said.

'Cheers. Is yours gin and tonic?'

'Vodka and tonic. Good for the breath. Something professionally I have to watch.'

Mother used to be good at placing people's accents and she had passed on some of her expertise to me. I guessed the woman was from London and more East End than Hampstead although she could have passed in Hampstead.

'How long have you been here?' I asked.

'In this flat? About two years.'

'You know the Addisons?'

'Yes.'

'Which is their flat?'

'Number twelve. You know them too, do you?'

'You've been well briefed.'

She reclined against the arm of a sofa. 'Sorry, I don't get it.'

'You say you bought it two years ago?'

'That's right.'

'Who sold it to you? Who was the vendor?'

She looked at me rather vacantly. 'Vendor? How should I know? I bought it through an agent. . . . Wait a sec. . . .' She closed her eyes, concentrating hard. Then her eyes opened wide and I noticed the irises were light blue. 'I do remember,' she said. 'It was an unusual name. Pencil, I think, or something very like. Pensman. Penman . . .'

She was very close to 'Pensom'.

'Pensom?' I asked.

She swung her arm and pointed a finger at me. 'Right! Do you know him too?'

'It happens to be my name.'

'I was going to ask what your name was.'

'It's my name and I haven't sold you my flat. Who's briefed you for this masquerade?'

'You are a funny man. Is this your usual line? It's a new one on me and I thought I'd heard them all.'

'It's no line.'

She smiled. 'No? I'm intrigued. Why pick on me? Have you seen me around and decided to chance it? Try your luck?'

'I've never seen you before in my life.'

A strange ugliness suddenly clouded her conventionally pretty features. Planes hardened and the cast of features became slightly twisted. If she'd been a dog she'd have been snarling.

'I hope you're not kinky,' she said harshly. 'A sneaky fetishist after my clothes basket. If so, you can finish your drink and get out quick. And don't try anything on. There are panic buttons all over the place and I'm right beside one.'

'The last thing I want to do is try something on,' I said scornfully. 'No way.'

The ugly look vanished; she became meltingly sweet; a

confection with a hard coating and a soft centre.

'You don't want to try something on?'

'I do not.'

'Then you won't want to take anything off, will you?'

She smothered a laugh. I knew she was mocking me and I wished I could say something cuttingly witty but I've never been much good at repartee. Anyway, my main thought was to find out why I was being persecuted, not to score points with flip come-backs.

'Have you eaten?' she asked.

Apart from a light meal on the aircraft I hadn't eaten since breakfast but I wasn't hungry. I was about to say so when she continued, 'I was just going to get something for myself when you came. And since you're here, and you seem trustworthy, would you care to stay for a meal? I can whip something up. No pun intended, none taken I hope.'

'I intend staying until I've found out what's going on.'

It sounded trite and laboured, but we were speaking different languages. I was being deadly serious and she was being light-hearted.

'I intend staying,' she mimicked. 'I like that. Masterful. I prefer Heathcliffs to Galahads every time.' She paused. 'Did you say your name was Pensom? What Pensom? Jasper? Sebastian?'

'Neil.' I adopted her Miss World style. 'I'm thirty-seven. Unmarried. Work as a television production assistant. Hobbies: collecting silver spoons and going to art exhibitions. Where are my spoons, by the way?'

Although I made it sound casual, I was more concerned about the whereabouts of my mother's collection than almost anything else. I could, of course, have walked out, gone to the police, and reported an intruder in my flat. But I reckoned if I did this she would have disappeared before the police arrived and I might not see her or my spoons again. Or find out who was responsible for this latest outrage affecting my personal life. For the time being my best bet was to stay cool and hope I could trap her into revealing who had hired her.

She ignored my question about the spoons. Instead, she said, 'Thirty-seven and unmarried, eh?' She gave a searching, penetrating look as though trying to see behind my eyes and into my mind. 'Are you gay?'

People think that if you've lived with your mother and haven't married you must be homosexual. Admittedly, she didn't know I'd lived with my mother – or perhaps she did – but her question didn't altogether surprise me. It had been raised more subtly on another occasion. The plain dull boring fact is that I'm not a particularly sexual creature. I've had my moments with women, not many, but with women, not men.

'No, I'm not gay.'

'Well, that's a relief. I don't want to waste my talents. Would you like me to rustle up something? I do a super baked fish with breadcrumbed clams.'

Again I wondered whether to go to the police and report trespass and theft, but again I decided to play along with whatever perverted game was being played – my gambler's instinct, I suppose! I said, 'That sounds good.'

'You can come with me to the kitchen while I get it ready. It's only common or garden coley and cod but I skin it first. Throw in bits of sliced onion, tomatoes, some herbs, milk, and put it in a casserole dish. The microwave does the rest.'

She came across and held out her hand. 'You're looking better. You went white as a sheet when you came in but you've got your colour back.'

I took her hand and let her lead me into my own kitchen. It hadn't been altered.

She was a jolie laide. One moment pretty, the next plain, but sexually attractive at all times. A natural wearer of the girdle of Venus. For some reason the phrase 'pillow talk' popped into my mind. If I could get her to pillow talk I might find out what the elaborate deception was about.

We chatted easily in the kitchen. I can't remember what we talked about but I began to feel comfortable. Perhaps I was relaxed by the brandy which she replenished periodically but I felt sure I would find out what evil genius was behind my abduction in a juggernaut, the fearsome Amanda, and now, the deprivation of my home by a sexy usurper. Pillow talk was the key.

We ate the meal in the kitchen and then she provided liver pâté which seemed an odd sequel. Next came slices of Swiss roll and thick Turkish coffee.

'Would you like some more?' she asked.

'No, thanks. I've had sufficient.'

She laughed. 'I've had sufficient,' she mimicked. 'Why don't you say "I've had enough."? What's this "sufficient"?'

She was right. I had adopted Mother's genteel way of speaking as my own.

'I've had enough,' I said.

'Great.'

We went into the living room or, as she called it, the lounge.

Another brandy was provided. I felt warm and comfortable and – it sounds crazy – I didn't object to being entertained as a stranger in my own flat.

I don't know how it happened, but it did happen. One minute I was talking about my curious adventures and the next she was sitting on my lap and we were kissing. From that to the bedroom was a short step. She insisted on keeping the lights on and momentarily this reminded me of the night with Amanda, but I didn't object.

It may be coy – it is certainly unfashionable – but I am not going to detail what I did, or she did, or we both did together in bed. Whatever was done, or not done, is a private matter between her and me.

When we were lying peacefully side by side I thought of

pillow talk. She was kissing the side of my face, my ear and the nape of my neck. The pupils of her eyes had enlarged and were a lustrous black rimmed by pale blue. I said, 'Who's behind this? Who's backing you?'

It was blunt, tactless and the worst possible thing to say. Even as I spoke I realised how crude it sounded. As a pillow-talker I scored zero out of ten.

'I think it's time for another drink,' she said. 'Do you want to stick to brandy or would you like tea or coffee?'

I knew I had blown it. 'Tea would be nice,' I said.

We dressed. As I slipped on my slacks I glanced around. We were in the second bedroom which I used as a guest room. It had a wash-basin and mirror and was next to the airing cupboard. But there were marks round the edge of the mirror and I didn't have to be Einstein to guess that in my absence a two-way mirror had been fixed and we had been filmed from a camera in the airing cupboard. For a moment, no longer, I toyed with the idea of exposing the fraud but if I had I would have ruined any chance of discovering the source of my persecution.

I was dressed before her and on my way to the living room I tried the door of the main bedroom, my bedroom. It was locked. It is a big enough room to take most of the furniture if carefully stacked and I guessed my furniture was inside.

As we drank tea she talked of her childhood. She had been born in Bermondsey and was one of a family of seven children, all girls. 'Dad gave up trying for a boy in the end.' From an early age she knew she possessed sex appeal; she also discovered it difficult to make permanent relationships. 'My trouble,' she said, 'is that when I'm with a man he's honestly the only man for me. But if I'm not with him, and I meet someone else who's got something different to offer, I'll stand up the first guy to try the second guy. I guess I'm amoral.'

I let her continue, feeding her with questions as if her

coming into the world ranked a close second to Christ's as the most important birth in history. And all the time I was thinking furiously why anyone should want to set me up for a sex pic. Blackmail was the first possibility, but I'm an unlucrative target. For extortion of this sort there must exist a person or people who would be hurt or shocked by revelation of one's intimate secrets. Now that Mother has gone I'm immune to this type of threat.

If it wasn't blackmail and I was simply to be an actor in a pornographic movie the result would be tame stuff. Such action as there was took place mostly under a thick bedspread. But from what I knew of the men who manipulated the sex-fantasy market it wouldn't be safe to make a fuss until I was sure of protection. For all I knew there was a hit man hiding in the airing cupboard who wouldn't take kindly to an intrusion. Not that I'm a coward but I don't believe in taking risks without first knowing the percentages. Apart from this, I'm very averse to physical violence.

The most likely explanation was that the staged seduction was part of an ongoing and expensive plan designed to make my life miserable. But why should anyone want this? I have no enemies, unless Marler can be counted as one, but ours is strictly a financial relationship and he'd have nothing to gain by driving me through a crazy obstacle course. It would be counter-productive to his interests.

Felicity had fallen silent. 'What are you thinking?' she asked.

'I was thinking about your life. It's been rather unhappy.'

'Not really. No more than most. Anyway, I believe *que sera, sera*. It's no use worrying. I guess I'm a fatalist. What will be, will be. I once knew a guy who thought it was all down to pyramids and . . .'

She was off again and I was free to analyse my dilemma. Without knowing the underlying reason for misfortunes since leaving Antwerp I was left to consider what my next move should be. Again I thought of going to the police and bringing the law into play. And again I realised that while I was trying to convince some hard-headed desk sergeant that I wasn't drunk or a nutter Felicity would be whisked away, my furniture restored, and by the time I turned up with police escort there would be nothing to corroborate my story. I should be accused of wasting police time and might even be arrested and have to spend a night in a cell. That would be a coup for my persecutor. No, I wouldn't go to the police. Not yet.

Felicity was coming to the end of her anecdote about a man who believed the secrets of the universe were related to the pyramids and slept in a bed covered by a pyramid-shaped canopy of butter muslin.

'Talking of beds,' I said (although I hadn't said a single word on the subject), 'I know it isn't late but I've got to think about a bed for tonight.'

She reached out and took my hand. 'You'll stay with me,' she said. 'Like I told you, I'm on my own tonight, and furthermore I like you. I quite fancy the quiet type. Still waters, and all that.'

To be honest, I quite liked her and in different circumstances would have been tempted to accept the invitation, but I'd formulated another plan. I would leave the flat and after making sure I wasn't being followed I'd make for a place where nobody would find me. I still had enough money to see me through a couple of days. I wouldn't even contact GLJ or anyone at Humberside. They might be wondering why I hadn't reported back but they'd have to wonder a little longer. Normally my professional life came before everything else, and normally I'd have reported back by now, but normality had deserted my life.

I took my hand from hers. 'Still waters get stagnant,' I said. 'Mine have got to start flowing again. I must go.'

'But where? According to you, I'm in your pad. So where

will you go?'

I felt fairly sure the place was bugged and all conversations were being recorded, and I had no intention of telling her or an unseen listener my plans.

'I shall stay with a friend.'

'A woman?' she asked with a smile.

'No. A man. A guy called Cedric.'

'Oh, and where does he live?'

'Islington.'

'I know Islington. Whereabouts?'

'Barnsbury Road.'

I did know someone who lived in Barnsbury Road but her name is Hilary and I had no intention of going there.

'Have another cup of tea. Have something stronger.'

'Thanks, but no. I've got to go.'

She tried every trick of seductive persuasion, cajoling and kissing, but the only thing that stiffened was my resolve.

I stood up and put on Hans's leather jacket.

'Thanks for the hospitality and next time I'm here I hope the furniture will be back in place. Incidentally, I know exactly how many spoons there should be. You can tell whoever's responsible . . .'

My farewell speech was interrupted by the doorbell.

'Just a sec,' she said. 'I'd better see who it is.'

The diversion was a godsend. And about time. God hadn't sent me much in the way of luck recently. If the unexpected caller was someone who knew me Felicity's game would be finished. I heard the door open and Felicity say in a surprised voice, 'Hello, Mum. What are you doing here?'

In her life story Felicity had mentioned her mother but I'd no idea she'd turn up here.

Felicity walked into the living room. 'Neil,' she said, 'I'd like you to meet my mother.'

Amanda entered, a Cheshire-cat smile on her face.

I would have bolted but her well-endowed body blocked

the doorway. It was the smile that faded away, not the Cheshire cat. The whiskers on her mole bristled. She wagged a finger at me. 'You naughty, wicked boy. And with my daughter too!' She turned to Felicity. 'I hope he's been behaving himself.'

'He's been a little bit naughty, Mum.'

'I suspected as much the moment I saw him. Guilt all over his face. It's as well I came when I did. Well, young man, what have you got to say for yourself?'

I'm unused to being called a young man and in a different context might have felt flattered. But the description was to my advantage. She couldn't claim to be my wife and Felicity's mother.

'At least you've dropped the pretence that we're married,' I said, moving forward. 'Now please let me pass.'

She continued to bar the way, arms akimbo. 'Pretence nothing. We were married at the registry office in Sevenoaks, as well you know. Three years ago. I agree that you might not have known Felicity was my daughter by my first marriage because she wasn't at the wedding or the reception. And you never did take much notice when I spoke about my girls, my seven bright diamonds, as I called them. But we're married all right even if it was only in a registry office. But I'm intending to put that right. I intend to have our union blessed.'

I looked at Felicity but she avoided my eyes.

'You should be ashamed,' I said angrily. 'How much are you being paid for this performance?'

She didn't answer.

I glanced at the window but reckoned the drop too far for safety. Inhibition prevented me from manhandling the woman. I would have to resort to subterfuge, but what subterfuge?

'Oh, yes,' said Amanda. 'I intend to have our marriage properly blessed. Why else do you think I've been chasing you over half Europe?'

91

I forced a smile. 'How did you know I was here?'

(It was a question I could have answered myself. She and her backers had obviously been listening into everything said and she'd been told to make an entrance when it was clear I was about to make an exit.)

'I always know where to find you, you naughty boy. You can't escape me.'

I went to the telephone.

'What are you doing now?' she demanded.

'Dialling nine-nine-nine. I want the fire brigade.'

'Fire brigade? Whatever for?'

'They have ladders. It's too far to jump. I'll leave by ladder.'

For a big woman she moved fast. 'You'll do nothing of the sort.' As she slapped her hand on the receiver rest to cut off the call, I dropped the phone, jinked round her like a rugby scrum half, and raced through the hall, out through the front door and to freedom.

In my haste I almost collided with a group of people getting out of the elevator. I glimpsed an astonished parson and some young women dressed to the nines. I swerved past them and raced down flights of stairs taking three at a time in reckless disregard of safety.

At the bottom of the stairs I paused and listened. No sign or sound of Felicity or her mother. I hurried out of the block and half-ran, half-walked to the nearest underground station. No doubt an accomplice posted outside the flats would try to follow me but it isn't difficult to give someone the slip if you know London's underground. My tormentors would probably make for Barnsbury Road, Islington. I was going to make for Brighton, a town with a high reputation for *chambres de passage*, anonymity and two casinos.

Within a couple of hours, and quite certain I hadn't been followed, I booked in at a hotel on the sea-front under the name of Brace, my mother's maiden name. I was given a room at the back with a fine view of a red brick wall but this didn't matter; I hadn't come on holiday. After a short catnap I ventured out to the promenade. It was now night. Lights glittered and winked along the front and a full moon threw a pale beam of light across the calm sea. My spirits rose. I was a free man. And then the bug began to bite, and bite hard. I felt certain I should be lucky tonight. It is a strangely thrilling feeling known only to those who have been captivated by the lure of the gaming table.

I walked through an unimposing entrance and was greeted by a receptionist who looked as if she might double during the day as a schoolgirl.

'Good evening, sir. Are you a member?'

'No, but I'll join.'

She reached for some papers. 'You'll need to fill in an application form. When your application has been approved you'll be able to enjoy yourself here.'

'I hope I'll be able to play tonight.'

'No, sir. You'll have to wait forty-eight hours. It's the law.'

Of course I knew it was the law but bribery usually worked.

I fished out a fiver and smuggled it into my fist which I reached out in the orthodox way of offering a tip while showing respect for the donee by not making the generosity look too obvious.

She jerked back as though I held a scorpion in my hand. Out of the corner of my eye I saw a figure looming in a shadowy background. She saw it too and relaxed. In a firm voice she said, 'I'm sorry, sir, but there's no way you can join the club and play tonight.'

The figure had now emerged from the shadows. It was a man. He wore a dinner jacket that was too small for his chest and a scarlet bow tie which was vulgarly large.

I stuffed the fiver back in my pocket. 'It's your loss,' I said loudly and left with as much dignity as I could muster.

Back at the hotel I chanced to get into conversation with

93

a man sitting at the bar who seemed to be on his own. After a few preliminaries – two dogs sniffing round each other – I confessed disappointment at having been refused entrance to the casino.

'You'd like to go?' he asked. 'I belong to both. You can come as my guest. I feel like a flutter. It's about time my luck changed.'

'Me too,' I said feelingly.

He slid off the bar-stool. 'I'm Bill Vickers. Call me Bill.'

'I'm Neil Pensom.' As I spoke I realised I'd given my true name and quickly added, 'Pensom-Brace, actually. But call me Neil.'

'Right, Neil. Let's go.'

I must say that British casinos, by and large, are shabby imitations of the continental and American ones I've patronised. They may have similar characteristics but the ceilings are generally too low for chandeliers, they are seldom decorated with bowls of flowers, the plush looks as if it was once a sale lot at a contents auction of a run-down stately home; they are tawdry and lack historic atmosphere.

Tonight I was determined not to go beyond a fixed limit, something which had been my downfall in the past. I consistently backed red and doubled up when I lost; very unadventurous but I made a bit and lost a bit as did my new-found friend. At one in the morning I felt suddenly overcome by fatigue and, as I was breaking even, I thought I'd call it a day. On other occasions I've been tired but pressed on. Sheer lack of will-power. But tonight my will-power was strong enough and that pleased me.

'Think I'll turn in, Bill,' I said.

'Sure,' he replied, without looking up from the table. 'Think I'll stay on. I'm getting lucky.'

'Good night then.'

Still without looking at me he said, 'Good night, Neil.'

I never saw him again.

Within a minute of climbing into bed I was asleep. I slept

without a break for nine hours and when I got up it was too late for breakfast at the hotel and so I took a stroll round the town, found a coffee shop and broke my fast there.

There is a similarity between intuition and inspiration. Both strike unexpectedly and both arrive like Minerva, fully formed. Both have to be grasped before they vanish. I didn't experience an intuition in the coffee shop but an inspiration struck.

I would call on Anthony, an old actor whom I'd known in my repertory days and who now lived alone in an apartment in Battersea. As I've always made a point of visiting him at Christmas I felt sure he'd let me stay with him until I got to the bottom of the whole rotten business which has made my life a misery. While there I would get everything down on paper before details slipped my memory. The notes I'd made in Hans's attic bedroom were in an inside breast pocket in my jacket. If by the time I'd written everything down I still had no idea of my persecutor's identity I would employ someone to help me.

So pleased was I with this plan that I would have left the shop without paying and had an embarrassing few moments convincing a sceptical cashier that it was pure oversight. I hurried to the railway station and caught the next train to London. After calling on my bank manager who grudgingly agreed to extend my overdraft I went straight to Anthony's apartment. As I'd expected, he was delighted to have company. Since the death of his live-in lover he's been very lonely. I told him some structural alterations were needed to my flat and I'd like to stay with him while workmen were on the job. There was no point in telling the truth. It wasn't simply that my strange experiences might have worried the old fellow, or even make him think some unknown disaster might strike us both; he is an incorrigible gossip and I didn't want him to blab my story around.

*　*　*

95

Samson closed the typescript and lighted up a cigar. While he smoked he thought about the story he had read and about the man who had brought it to him. Pensom seemed quiet and inoffensive but long ago Samson had learned not to trust appearances. Docile exteriors sometimes concealed devious minds and violent emotions.

After a while he got up and went to the chair where Pensom had been sitting. He felt under and all around it. Next he went to his desk and repeated the operation. He went all round the room checking under surfaces.

Shandy was flicking through papers in the filing cabinet when he entered the outer office. 'Finished?' she asked.

He put a finger to his mouth in a silencing gesture.

She raised her eyebrows and resumed her search for a file.

Samson prowled round the office feeling under flat surfaces and examining various fittings. In the end he asked, 'Were you in the room all the time with Pensom?'

'No. I left him to come and tell you he'd arrived without an appointment. You were practising thin smiles at the time.'

Samson examined the telephone and all other equipment. Eventually he said, 'It seems clean.'

'You think he might have planted a bug?'

'He or someone might have.'

She took a file from the cabinet and shut the drawer. 'There's nothing inside that,' she said.

'I hope not. It should be kept locked at all times when not in use.'

'Yes, sir.'

Her mock deference didn't raise a smile, as it sometimes did, from Samson. 'When games are being played,' he said, 'and I think Pensom is part of a very strange game, and I'm drawn into that game, I like to know the rules. When I don't know the rules I stick to my own rules, and the first, before all others, is to check my own security. Now I'm going out for a breath of fresh air and another check.' He tossed the typescript onto her desk. 'I'd like you to read that while I'm out.'

The street was crowded with afternoon shoppers. Heat beat off the pavements and the faint smell of road tar mingled with the fumes of vehicle exhausts. Samson turned up a pedestrian precinct lined with the stalls of market traders. Different smells prevailed here: fruit and vegetables, clothing fabrics, snatches of perfume, the sharp notes of hamburgers and onions as well as the spoors of personal odours that weaved through all the other smells.

Every so often he paused to examine articles on a stall and glance behind him. Slowly he progressed to the far end of the market, crossed another street and came to a square where sun-burned grass was littered with candy-bar wrappings and empty crisp packets. The half-dozen benches round the perimeter of the square were occupied by people in various degrees of undress basking in the sun. A loose dog lifted its leg against a dusty bush and a sparrow flew between two trees with splintered trunks. Their lower branches had been torn off by vandals.

Samson stood in the centre of the square surveying the scene. No one had tailed him. Then he made his way back to his office, pausing at a stall that had a miscellany of old clocks and watches for sale. His expert eye roved across the display but there was nothing of value for his collection. When he reached the door that led up some stairs to his office he stopped and looked at the bustling street scene and he glanced up at the building opposite where there were vacant office premises and a flat. He decided to increase his offer by a thousand pounds; then he left the heat of the street to mount the stairway and enter cooler surroundings.

Shandy was bent over the typescript.

'Haven't you finished it yet?'

'Give us a chance.'

'Thought you were a quick reader. Anything come up while I was out?'

'It's August. Nothing much ever happens in August.'

He nodded. 'That's right. If people go missing in August other people don't seem to notice. It's after the holidays that people notice someone or something is missing and adulteries are confessed or found out. . . . When you've finished, let me know.'

'Right.'

In his room Samson went to the bookshelf behind his desk and took out an atlas. He turned to the page showing a map of south-west Germany and eastern France. Pensom had travelled from Baden-Baden to Stuttgart, changing at Karlsruhe. But the airport at Strasbourg was nearer than Stuttgart, so why had he gone to Stuttgart? Because he hadn't wanted to cross a frontier?

After putting back the atlas he ran through the tape of his comments on the typescript. None of these amounted to much and there was no common denominator; yet he felt sure that somewhere in the narrative was an invisible linking thread. For a while he sat with his eyes closed. For some reason his mind kept returning to Hans Vogel's early-morning jog. It wasn't merely that it seemed very unusual for a keen jogger to be a heavy smoker, something else teased the corners of Samson's mind, something not quite right, not in keeping.

At the top of a hill, a statue of Meister Erwin standing in front of a semi-circle of locust trees. A cemetery on the slope of the hill. Well-tended graves and a gardener's hut. A village nestling in a hollow. A church spire, a row of poplars and a single factory chimney stack. Given that the chimney was in keeping with the village because it belonged to a brick foundry; and given that the statue was in keeping because Meister Erwin was Steinbach's most famous native; given that German communities probably looked after grave spaces better than the British, what else didn't fit, wasn't in keeping? Only the gardener's hut.

Possibly all German cemeteries had such huts and yet one would expect to find any hut, or building connected with the cemetery, near the entrance to the burial ground, close to habitation, not tucked away in a far corner. The hut was in the wrong place.

The intercom buzzed. Shandy's voice came through. 'I've finished.'

'I'll be with you.'

'You don't want me to bring it in?'

'No, thanks.'

Samson closed the inter-connecting door and drew up a chair beside her. 'Well?' he asked.

'It's entertaining enough. As a mystery story. But what's the purpose of it all?'

'That's what I intend to find out.'

'You're taking it on then?'

'Yes.'

She gave him a quick, approving look. She liked it when her boss got his teeth into a case. He was lazy by nature and recently had become increasingly bored with his job. Only a few days before he had said, 'I'm sick of serving writs on people who don't want to be served, of tracing people who don't want to be found, of advising on security to people who don't want to pay the cost of what I recommend, of barging into places where I'm not wanted, of being regarded as a cross between a strong-arm gorilla and a down-at-heel snooper. . . .'

Her approving look was reflected in a softer tone of voice. 'Any ideas?'

'Everywhere he went there were facilities to film him and record anything spoken. He was filmed in the streets of Antwerp, there were stills taken in Rubens House, he could have been filmed from the restaurant by the ferry at Breskens, he was filmed in the juggernaut, probably an infra-red camera recorded him being dumped by the statue, and then – and this is what put me on to the thread which runs through it all – he was undoubtedly filmed from the gardener's hut by the cemetery. It wouldn't surprise me if the hut wasn't rigged up for the purpose and dismantled as soon as he'd been "found" by Herr Vogel.'

'So Vogel was in on the act?'

'I'd guess so. When Pensom shouted to him he didn't hear at first. Pensom shouted again and Vogel stopped close to the hut. Hidden cameras could have filmed the Vogel's living room and the bedroom. I doubt if he was filmed on his way back to England but certainly he was when he found a young woman in occupation of his flat.'

'It figures,' said Shandy. 'What's the next move?'

'I'd like you to book me on the next flight to Strasbourg and make sure a hire car is waiting for me.'

'Will do. Why Strasbourg and not Stuttgart?'

Beneath drooping eyelids Samson's eyes twinkled. 'Two reasons. One, it's nearer to Steinbach than Stuttgart, but, far more important, I'll be able to visit a place I've wanted to visit for a long time. The cathedral.'

'The cathedral?' she exclaimed. 'Since when have you been interested in ecclesiastical architecture, or religion for that matter?'

'It's a clock.' Animation came to his heavy features. 'It's a clock I've wanted to see for years.'

'What does it do apart from tell the time? Pop out storks with bundles in their beaks?'

'It's an astronomical clock inside the cathedral. At twelve-thirty every day mechanical figures of the twelve disciples pass before the figure of Christ and are blessed by him. This happens in complete silence but after the last blessing a mechanical cock crows and flaps its wings. And that's not all. Below this scene there is another play being enacted all about death and the ages of Man.'

'Interesting.'

Samson snorted. 'Interesting! I'll say it is. Legend has it

that when the clock had been installed the magistrates of Strasbourg decided it should be the only one of its sort in the world. So they accused the clock-maker of witchcraft and said he must have been united with the Devil to have created such a wonderful work of art. The poor chap was thrown into prison and condemned to be blinded.'

'Charming! You watch it when you go there. Incidentally, why go all the way to Germany to check out Pensom? Why not start here with his flat and the woman who's taken it over?'

'Do you know the address of the flat?'

She thought. 'He gave me an address in Battersea, care of Mr A Vestier, a friend of his.'

'Exactly. But his own flat is in Dulwich. Or so he said. I should have got the address from him.' Samson sighed. 'I slipped up there.'

'I can check the electoral register.'

'He won't be on it yet. He's only been there a couple of months. Anyway, I don't want to go to Dulwich. I want to go to Strasbourg.'

'So is this jaunt business or pleasure? Does it go down on his expenses?'

'You're being difficult.'

Shandy laughed. 'Not really. I'd just like to hear what you thought of Felicity Flowerdew, if you could find her.' She turned to a micro-computer and keyed a number. From information on the VDU she keyed another number and obtained the flight times of aircraft travelling from England to Strasbourg. 'Air France have a flight from Heathrow at ten-fifteen tomorrow,' she said. 'Would that suit?'

'Fine.'

'And what do I tell Pensom if he calls while you're away?'

'Tell him I've had to go to Scotland but should be back the following day and I've taken his fascinating story to read on the train.'

She picked up the phone. 'I'll see if there's a seat available tomorrow.'

Samson waited while she booked him on the flight. Another call ensured that a self-drive car would be waiting at the airport.

'What do you expect to find in Steinbach?' she asked.

'A cemetery with or without a gardener's hut. I shall nose around. See what I can find out about the Vogels. Maybe call on them.'

'And then what?'

'I shall play it by ear.' He paused, deep in thought. 'I wish I knew more about Marler. Pensom is afraid of him and he belongs to a part of Pensom's life which he regrets. We know he has a weakness for gambling. It could be that he owes money to Marler. But then he's ruled out Marler as being behind this peculiar sort of harassment. Reckons it would be counter-productive for Marler to persecute him.' Samson stood up. 'I've got a little job for you tomorrow while I'm away.'

'Oh, yes? What?'

'Try to find out what you can about Lloyd Jackson. What his hobbies or interests are, anything.'

'Do you think he's involved in this?'

'That's a good question but not the best question.'

Shandy leaned back in her chair and looked up at him. 'What is the best question, Mr Samson?'

'The best question is – why should anyone want to spend a hell of a lot of money hounding a man as ordinary as Neil Pensom?'

SOME PREDATORS ARE MALE
Part 4

Samson parked his car close to a bridge spanning the river that meanders through the heart of Strasbourg. From here he could see the rose-tinted cathedral spire soaring above half-timbered riverside buildings that had steep medieval roofs encrusted with tiny dormer windows. For a few moments he stood, dwelling on the scene. Waterscapes, whether they were rivers, harbours or the open sea, were a source of pleasure, and in contemplating them he came as near as it was possible for him to attain inner peace.

For these few seconds his mission to Steinbach, and the immediate objective of seeing the cathedral's astrological clock, were forgotten. Even the noise of traffic and the movement of pedestrians didn't distract him. Briefly he was part of the timelessness of Time, sometimes called universal harmony, which to him was more deity than the God worshipped in churches and cathedrals.

The spell of inner peace soon passed and he was once again a fat man in a strange city. He crossed the bridge and made his way down nearly deserted streets towards the cathedral. As he turned into the *rue des Ecrivans*, and he noticed the street's name on a blue plaque attached to the side of a building, he thought of the writer whose story he'd left in the car. Neil Pensom had claimed a good knowledge of French but only a smattering of German. Yet in his narrative German phrases, not included in tourists' phrase books, were correctly used. *Rue des Ecrivans* – street of writers; was there more than one author involved in the story?

In the cathedral he joined a cluster of tourists, many equipped with flash-bulb cameras, and watched mechanical disciples receive a mechanical blessing. He was deeply impressed by the skill of the craftsman who had constructed the entertaining clock and it struck him as symbolically apt that the blessings should be so mechanical. On his way out he didn't buy a candle to light to add to the hundreds of other candles which were the only illumination of a gloomy interior, but he did purchase a booklet about the history of the cathedral. Standing outside, in a square pullulating with human activity, he skimmed through the booklet and saw a reference to Meister Erwin. There was a statue of the architect outside one of the cathedral walls.

It was easy to find. The expression on Meister Erwin's face looked as if he had been sculpted while sucking a lemon. Pensom had mentioned a disdainful expression on the face of the Steinbach statue. Perhaps, thought Samson, he realised that designing buildings for the glory of God was of less practical value than designing buildings for habitation. Man might not live by bread alone, but bread was the top priority.

After some reflections about mankind's need to worship, whether it was an intangible force or a graven image, Samson strolled across the cathedral square to a large well-preserved medieval house, the Maison Kammerzell, which had been converted into a restaurant and was renowned for its cuisine. A resolution to lose weight was temporarily erased as he studied the menu. He ordered *Sauerbraten* served with potato pancakes and followed this with *Mürbeteig*, a sweet dessert pastry. Shandy would not approve, but it would be his only meal that day.

In mid-afternoon he ambled back to his car and studied a road map. The Rhine, a short distance to the east, formed a natural boundary between France and Germany. A few miles further on he would reach the autobahn which ran between Basel and Frankfurt. Baden-Baden was fairly close

106

to the autobahn and Samson reckoned he could be there within an hour.

Like Pensom, he found Baden-Baden larger and more crowded than he'd anticipated. He threaded his way through the town and took the road leading to the south-east. After passing a complex of radio and television studios on the left and a golf course on the right he entered the fringe of the Black Forest. But soon he was in open country and heading towards the village of Steinbach. It was then that he began to regret having lunched so well after a period of comparative abstinence. A burning sensation in his gullet warned him he was going to be attacked by indigestion. He thought of Shandy again and could almost hear her saying, 'Serves you right.' It seemed unfair that he should get indigestion during a course of dieting when he'd hardly ever suffered through eating whatever he fancied.

When he arrived at the village he pulled up by an inn and got out of the car. A small stream ran beside the road and for a few moments Samson leaned on a stone parapet gazing at its slow running water and a hedgerow beyond. The break, with some deep breathing, eased his indigestion and he began to concentrate on the task in hand. His first step would be to find the cemetery and check whether there was a gardener's hut at the top. Then he would try to locate the Vogels' house by following Pensom's description of the route from cemetery to house.

Back in the car he read through parts of the typescript and then drove off the main road and up a street that appeared to lead to the centre of the village. Like most small villages in the region the buildings were perfectly maintained, and many were embellished by window-boxes packed with geraniums and other flowers. The few shops didn't exhibit their wares brashly but preferred to have window displays discreetly set back behind wide porticoes. One of the stores had an elegantly designed fresco above

107

the entrance. Against peach-wash plaster background it showed a tall thin figure of a man in medieval garb and next to him but in fainter outline as if to give a perspective of distance the outline of a cathedral tower and spire. Beneath this art work were the words *Meister Erwin Apotheke*. If Samson hadn't known he was in Steinbach before, he knew it now. No one who came this way could deny the pride of a village in its most famous son.

Samson parked his car in the shade of a tall linden tree and climbed out. It was another hot day and as he walked to the chemist's shop he took the shady side of the street. He had a fair grasp of German but the word for indigestion, *das Verdauungsmangel*, wasn't easy to remember and he muttered it to himself as he walked.

It was cooler inside the store. After purchasing tablets he enquired the way to the cemetery. It wasn't far, the woman behind the counter assured him, about half a kilometre and up the hill past the church. Samson put the bottle of tablets in the leather case containing Pensom's typescript and, although it was hot, he decided to walk. By the time he reached the cemetery entrance he was mopping his forehead with a handkerchief. He trod between meticulously kept grave-spaces, bowing his head as he passed two mourners kneeling before a marble tombstone. It wasn't a very large burial ground and almost at once he realised that if there had ever been a gardener's hut it had now disappeared. And when he reached the top and scanned the perimeter he couldn't find any trace that a hut had once stood there.

Having come this far he walked the few extra paces to look at the figure doomed forever to gaze stonily westwards towards Strasbourg. It was a peaceful setting, distant but not too far distant from human habitation, but why, Samson wondered, had this place, of all places, been chosen as the spot to abandon Neil Pensom? The obvious answer was that it was close to the home of the man who would

108

'discover' him and was almost certainly an accomplice in the plot. But plot for what purpose? Why go to such extravagant lengths to disturb and disorientate someone who couldn't afford to buy himself out of trouble and had no enemies except possibly a man called Marler.

Thoughtfully Samson proceeded to follow the route taken by Pensom and Hans Vogel. At a gate he unzipped his case and took out the typescript. Reading the account of the walk between the monument and Vogel's house Samson was struck by the explicit nature of the directions. It was almost as if, when writing, Pensom had deliberately made the route clear to anyone who might read his story.

A suspicious scout of the subconscious which had patrolled the back of Samson's mind once again presented itself for inspection. Was he too being set up as a player in the charade? Had he really been picked at random from the Yellow Pages?

A cooling breeze blew across the hill and as he rested by the gate it occurred to him that he and Pensom had something in common. Neither had close relatives and both lived alone. Not a bad idea, he thought grimly, if you are going to play games with the lives of other people to select individuals where no familial tears would be shed if the game went tragically wrong.

He opened the typescript. It was clear that during Pensom's walk the brickworks were on the left; this meant he, Samson, should turn right at the lane. He walked past small orchards, plots growing garden produce, a vineyard, and finally an unfenced orchard which had trees laden with ripe plums. This must be the property of the advocate whose wife made delicious plum tarts. Samson resisted the temptation to pick a plum; he didn't want to reactivate the bout of indigestion.

Turning into another lane he saw a house that had windows lying flush with a red-tiled roof. Part of the house was screened by trees. Close to the house was a tamarisk-like tree which bore a profusion of red berries. Samson had no doubt he was approaching the Vogels' house. It stood on the corner where the lane joined a wider road.

According to Pensom's account the Vogels had been due to visit England for an excursion to Stratford-upon-Avon with a group of boys. He mounted stone steps leading to the front door and rang a bell. From within came the sound of musical chimes. He waited and rang again. More chimes, but nobody came to answer the call. Samson retreated down the steps and looked up. All windows were securely closed, a sure sign on a hot summer's day that the occupants weren't at home.

The house faced a road which had other houses on either side. These were well spaced. Mature trees and hedges marked territorial boundaries. Samson strolled down the road hoping to meet someone who would know the Vogels and where he might find them. In the front garden of the next-but-one house a woman wearing a coloured cotton blouse, orange shorts and flat sandals was snipping with secateurs at a bush. She wore a floppy hat and dark sunglasses; Samson estimated her age as forty-plus.

He decided the time had come to polish up his rusty conversational German. 'Excuse me,' he said, and his voice sounded as though sandpaper had stuck in his throat, 'but I am looking for friends I once met on holiday. The Vogels. Do you know them?'

The woman stopped her work and came over to him. She took off her sunglasses. 'Yes, I know them. You say you met them on holiday?'

'Yes, in England. I'm English. We exchanged addresses but I lost theirs. I remembered it was Steinbach and someone in the village directed me up here.'

The woman gave a broad smile. 'Your German is not so good, if I may say so. Shall we speak English? I think mine will pass the test.'

'With pleasure. Which is the Vogels' house?'

110

The woman pointed. 'That one. If you came up from the village you passed it. But you're out of luck. They're on holiday.'

Samson assumed an expression of disappointment. 'What a pity. I'm sorry to have missed them. Is it England again? I know Hans likes it.'

The woman laughed, 'And so does Gerda, but for different reasons. Are you staying here or just passing through?'

'Just passing through. I thought I'd look them up.'

The woman glanced up and down the road. 'You came by car?'

'I parked it in the village.' Samson mopped his brow. 'That was a mistake. It's too hot for walking.'

She narrowed her eyes, scrutinising him, and for a moment Samson wondered if she'd seen through his deception. But she was merely weighing up whether it was safe to invite a stranger into her house for a cooling drink.

'I don't know you,' she said, 'and one has to be careful these days but Hans and Gerda would never forgive me if I didn't offer you a little hospitality. Would you like to come in? I have beer in the refrigerator or a soft drink if you would prefer it.'

'A beer sounds marvellous.'

'Good. Come along in then. Everyone round here seems to be on holiday. I shall be glad of some company.'

Indoors, she led the way to a room which had rush-mats on a pale green thermoplastic-tile floor. 'I call this the Egyptian room. My late husband and I lived in Egypt for five years. He was an embassy official. Sit down. I'll get you a beer.'

Samson chose a chair with carved jackal heads on its armrests. Pinewood walls were covered with paintings and photographs of Egyptian scenes. A huge bronze bust of Nefertiti stood on a corner cabinet and the firescreen in front of a brick fireplace depicted two-dimensional figures and was a copy of a typical Egyptian frieze or temple bas-relief. But the strangest furnishing was a complete sarcophagus standing in the opposite corner from the Nefertiti bust. It was in stone and sculpted in the likeness of Tutankhamun but the beard was broken off and only traces of lapis lazuli and gold leaf remained.

The woman returned carrying a marquetry tray in which slivers of ivory, bone and mother-of-pearl were set in wood of various shades. 'This shows Nekhebet, the protective goddess of Upper Egypt, in the form of a vulture hovering over the head of a Pharaoh. But I expect at the moment you're more interested in quenching your thirst.' She placed a glass of beer on a table beside Samson and went with her own glass to sit near the bust. 'Good health,' she said.

'Good health.'

'My name is Eva Grunblatt. And you?'

'John Spencer,' he replied without hesitation.

She looked thoughtful. 'Spencer? Spencer? Not the same as . . . Am I right . . . I read all the gossip. Our magazines love your royal family.'

'I may be distantly related to the well-known Spencers,' said Samson grandly.

'How exciting,' she beamed. 'Did Hans and Gerda know that?'

'I don't think so. Has Hans taken a party of boys with him?'

'Oh, yes. He will be touring famous places.'

'And Gerda?'

Eva Grunblatt chuckled. 'That's a different story.'

Samson took a chance, a shot in the dark. 'I guessed she had another interest in London,' he said, and winked.

The wink scored. 'Yes, and why not, I say. Here, she is the perfect housewife. Elsewhere, perhaps not. But Hans doesn't object. After all, most of the year he gets treated like a pasha. But I mustn't gossip. Are you on holiday, Mr

Spencer, or business?'

'Holiday. A motoring holiday. I decided to travel along the Rhine putting up on spec each night. As I was close to Steinbach I thought I'd make a diversion.'

'You have been to Germany before?'

'Yes. I like it here.'

'Might I ask, what is your business?'

Samson used a cover he had adopted before. It was a trade in which even an expert couldn't trap him. 'I deal in old clocks and timepieces. As a lover of Egyptology you will know the ancient Egyptians were among the pioneers of telling the time.'

'Yes, indeed. From shadows thrown by obelisks. There is one still at Karnak. You have its sister by the river Thames in London.'

'And you?' Samson enquired. 'Do you have any business interests?'

She shook her head. 'I don't do much these days. You might not believe it but when I was younger I was in demand as an actress. But that finished when I got married although since my husband died I have managed to get a few acting parts again. Bit parts I think you call them. I did a commercial recently where I had to make myself look a fool in front of a washing machine.' She laughed. 'I don't mind. It brings in some money. Not that I am short. I have a good widow's pension. Friends think this house is too big for me but I don't see why I should move to a smaller one if I like it here and can afford to keep it up, do you?'

'I don't,' said Samson. 'Why move if you don't have to.' As he spoke he thought of his own prospective move to the premises across the street. 'I'd only move if there were distinct advantages.'

'Exactly what I say.'

'You enjoy acting?' he asked.

'Oh, yes. Very much.' She became coy. 'I have a book of cuttings. Would you like to see it?'

113

'I would.'

She left the room and returned with a large album bound in red leather.

'I shouldn't be showing off like this,' she said with an apologetic giggle, 'but a little vanity never did anyone harm. And I'm quite proud of how I looked when I was young and slim.'

Photographs were interspersed with newspaper cuttings. In the early pictures Eva Grunblatt justified her boast.

'I put on weight in my early twenties and a lot more after marriage . . . Don't look at those. They aren't so good.' She made a move to take away the album.

Samson was gazing at a gloss photograph of a woman in eighteenth-century costume with a high, powdered wig on her head. An enormous patch on her left cheek looked like a parody of the fashionable beauty spot of the period. Hairs sprouted from the artificial mole.

'Don't look at that, please.' Eva Grunblatt took the album from his hands. 'There was a series of short films for children about popular folk tales. The Frenchman Perrault got the credit for most of them but this one, like many others, was an old German folk tale before Perrault was born.'

'What part were you playing?' Samson asked.

'An ugly step-sister in Cinderella. Couldn't you guess?'

Samson felt exultant. He knew he had found Pensom's Amanda. He said, 'The picture doesn't do you credit.' Then he tried another shot in the dark. 'Speaking of pretty women, has Gerda Vogel done any acting?'

'No. But for a while she worked in our local television station as a secretary. That's how she first met' – she cut off the sentence and slapped her own wrist – 'stop gossiping, Eva.'

'You were going to say that's how she met someone who became a very good friend, a friend of the family, so to speak.'

114

'Well, yes. But I didn't say it. Not that I blame her. He is quite flamboyant. A character.'

'Actors often are,' said Samson.

'Not an actor,' she corrected. 'A director. Television mostly although I think he has produced a movie.'

'Most people in the entertainment industry are larger than life.'

'Larger than life!' She slapped her thigh. 'I'm larger than life, yes?'

'I didn't mean . . .'

'Oh, I don't mind. You're a big man yourself. Do you mind?'

'Not a bit.'

'And nor do I. I don't envy little Gerda in the least. Less of her and she'd vanish into thin air. But I expect that suits her friend. He is on the short side himself.' She looked appraisingly at Samson. 'My husband was a big man, not unlike you. He was a good wrestler. Graeco-Roman style. It was his relaxation. Do you wrestle, Mr Spencer?'

'I can, but boxing was my first choice as a young man,' said Samson truthfully. He took a long drink of beer. Eva Grunblatt was staring at him in a disconcerting way rather as if he were an outsize melon she was considering slicing into for that evening's hors d'oeuvres. He could understand why Pensom had felt threatened by the sight of her in a pink nightdress.

'The fashion nowadays is for sticks of women,' she said. 'I should have lived in the days when women painted by Rubens were prized.'

'You're interested in art?' asked Samson putting down an empty glass.

'Yes and no. Some art. Recently I visited Rubens House in Antwerp. Have you been there?'

'Not to Rubens House, but I've been to Antwerp. There's a magnificent clock in Central Station.'

Eva Grunblatt half-rose from her chair. 'I have an old

115

clock. I think it may be valuable. May I show it to you?'

'By all means.'

'Excuse me a moment.' She stood up, tugged at her shorts which had stuck to her thighs, and left the room.

Samson decided he'd leave as soon as he'd seen the clock. He'd already learned a great deal and was unlikely to find out much more without arousing suspicion. When Eva Grunblatt returned she was carrying a wooden clock which, above the dial, had the figure of a man holding a cord. She removed Samson's glass and placed the clock gently on the table.

'Would you like another beer?'

'No, thanks.' He picked up the clock and in the manner of an expert valuer certain that his opinion is beyond contradiction stated, 'This was made in the Black Forest.'

'I believe so.'

'Sometimes called a Dutch clock.' Samson paused. 'It's in good condition. Have you had it long?'

'It's been in my family over a hundred years. They say my great-grandfather made it. He was a farmer.'

Samson nodded. 'Farmer-clockmakers were fairly common at one time. They carried them round in special packs on their backs. All the parts, including toothed wheels, were made of wood. The bells were made of glass. That little fellow' – he indicated the figure above the dial – 'pulls the cord every half-hour. Right?'

'Not now. It needs some repair.' She gave him an admiring look. 'You know your job, Mr Spencer.'

Samson gave a modest smile. 'The Black Forest clock industry is famous. Incidentally, the cuckoo clock came from the Black Forest, not Switzerland. But then a lot of good things come from this region. The wine, the cherry cream cake.'

Her eyes lighted. 'You like *kirschtorte?*'

'I do.'

'Then you shall have a piece.'

116

Samson placed the clock on the table. 'It's very kind of you but I must be on my way.' He stood up.

'Must you really go? I'm enjoying your company.'

'I'm afraid so. But thank you for the beer.'

'I'll tell Hans and Gerda you called. They'll be sorry to have missed you. . . . My clock. Would it fetch much in London?'

'Hard to say. It's not in full working order although in good condition. You should get a few hundred pounds.'

'How about a slice of my cake to take with you?' she asked. Before he could reply she said, 'I'll go and cut a piece for you.'

Samson didn't detain her: there was no false social grace about not wishing to put her to the trouble, or saying 'If you insist . . .' His indigestion had gone and the resolution to diet hadn't yet returned.

She brought in a wedge of cake carefully wrapped in clingfilm. He opened his case and put it in with the tablets and typescript.

She watched him with round eyes. 'Don't crush it, Mr Spencer. I'll get a box to put it in.'

'I'll take care of it,' he said. 'I'll treat it like a baby. Thank you again, Frau Grunblatt.' He gave a formal bow.

'It was my pleasure, and should you be this way again . . .'

'I'll make sure to see you.' Samson had now edged his way to the hall.

'By the way, what passed between us is confidential, Mr Spencer. I wouldn't like my good friends to think I discuss them behind their backs.'

Samson decided to take one more chance, one more shot in the dark. Eva Grunblatt was obviously in the cast-list of the plot against Pensom. Hans and Gerda Vogel were also implicated. Gerda was having some sort of affair with a television director. Could that director be Geraint Lloyd Jackson?

117

'Have no fear,' he said. 'I won't breathe a word. Anyway, I had a good idea of the state of things. While I was with them Gerda had a telephone call from someone called Jackling, Jackson or Jackman. Some such name.'

A change came over her. 'You have an exceptionally good memory, Mr Spencer. Where were you all when this call came through?'

Samson realised he had gone too far. She was suspicious. And her question put him on the spot. Having proved he possessed a good memory he could hardly say he couldn't remember where the call was received.

'We were having a drink in a hotel bar.'

'Very strange. Normally Gerda doesn't like drinking in public.'

He made it to the front door. 'Well, it's neither here nor there, is it? Their business entirely. Good day, Frau Grunblatt.'

'Where are you heading for now?'

Out of the corner of his eye he saw her pick up something from a hatstand. 'Koblenz,' he said, stepping forward. 'Good day.'

He was about five paces down the garden path when she called, 'Mr Spencer!'

He turned to see her holding a small camera to her eye. A shutter clicked.

'Good,' she said. 'The Vogels will be delighted to see this. Proof that you called to see them. Good day, Mr Spencer.'

It was still very hot but he scarcely noticed the heat. He was recapitulating everything that had been said and wondering whether, apart from the slip about Jackson, he'd made mistakes. In any event, she might contact Jackson, or the Vogels, or both. There wouldn't be time to transmit a copy of the photograph but she could give a physical description. He would be watchful when he arrived back at Heathrow. But even if the person who was masterminding

118

the operation learned Pensom had employed a private detective it wouldn't matter so long as Pensom's hideaway wasn't discovered.

It was early evening as he drove to Strasbourg and it was necessary to pull down the sun-shield as the sun was shining almost directly into his eyes. It had been a productive day. First, he'd seen the clock in Strasbourg Cathedral; next, ascertained that no gardener's hut existed; and finally obtained useful information from Eva Grunblatt. There was clearly a connection, in more sense than one, between the Vogels and a television director who had sent his assistant to look for locations in Belgium and Holland. Samson felt confident he'd soon have the case wrapped up. And then what? He would collect his fee, but what would Pensom do?

In English law there were no grounds for bringing an action against someone for causing mental distress. In fact, provided no law was broken, and no physical damage inflicted, people could persecute one another as much as they wished, and they frequently did. Some persecution was unintentional, but persecution nevertheless; and some victims suffered not from a real persecutor but from their own disturbed imaginations and were labelled paranoic.

Was Pensom the victim of a complex persecution or a persecution complex? Persecution and paranoia were everywhere and, in one form or another, to be found in almost every family unit. Which family, Samson wondered, doesn't have its domestic tyrant? Perhaps Pensom's mother was one but Pensom himself wasn't paranoic. He was a victim and it was unlikely that he had any legal remedy against his victimiser.

No criminal offence had been committed in England and, as for the abduction in Antwerp, he would need to consult a specialist in international law, a costly and time-consuming exercise. So what had he to gain if his persecutor was identified? He could go to a lawyer and obtain an interim

119

injunction pending formulation of a case for nuisance or some other tort, but this was a tricky area of law in which plaintiffs had to risk paying heavy legal fees and maybe receive only minimal damages. Besides, Pensom seemed chronically in debt and unless he could get legal aid most lawyers would be wary of instituting proceedings without being confident of success. But this was Pensom's problem and didn't arise until the name and motive of the persecutor were known, and name and motive were Samson's problem.

He always travelled first-class on flights, not for status or to bump up expense accounts, but because the food was better in the first-class cabin and, more important, the spacious seats accommodated his avoirdupois. Today, with an effort of will, he waved away a tray offered by an air hostess. His resolution to diet had been reaffirmed.

At Heathrow he walked through the 'Nothing to declare' corridor and out into the general concourse. There was the usual line of people waiting for friends or relatives and the usual number of people meeting strangers and holding up cards with a surname printed on them. But among the hopefuls waiting for travellers to arrive was a man with a cine-camera. Samson might have ignored him except that the camera swung to follow as he moved past. He continued on his way, walked through the electrically controlled door of one exit and immediately came back again through a different entrance. He saw the man with the cine-camera hurrying away.

Samson followed him into the multi-storey car park and as the man was unlocking the door of a Ford Granada Samson seized his free arm in a paralysing grip, pinching the upper arm at a point which gave maximum pain. As the man swung round to face the attack Samson used his weight as a weapon and pinned him against the car.

'What the hell . . .'

'Right,' said Samson grimly. 'What the hell are you

120

doing taking camera shots of me?'

'I wasn't doing any such thing. Let me go.'

Without releasing the arm with its nerves painfully trapped Samson shoved his bulk into the man making him a sandwich filling. 'Who sent you?'

'I don't know what you're talking about.'

Samson heard footsteps approaching, high heels clicking on concrete. A woman was going to a parked car. He knew she would soon be within vision. With his free hand he grabbed the camera and without taking his eyes from the man who was gasping for breath, opened the camera and exposed the film.

'Christ,' moaned the man. 'What's the idea, you bastard, you?'

'Tell your boss not to play games with me.' Samson dropped the camera, stood back and gave the man's face a playful slap.

The footsteps were close. Samson walked away. A voice came after him. 'You'll be sorry!'

Samson sidestepped to avoid a woman who gave him a freezingly angry look.

A minute later he was at the taxi rank and hiring a cab to take him home, satisfied that his suspicions had been confirmed. Eva Grunblatt must have contacted someone who had arranged for his arrival at Heathrow to be filmed.

After a quick wash and change of clothes he poured a stiff whisky. Then he switched on the answerphone. Shandy's voice came through.

'Welcome back. Hope you had a lovely holiday. What did you bring me? Duty-free scent? Wine from Alsace? Something nice, I'm sure. While you've been swanning around, I've been busy. I closed the office, hung a notice on the door saying "Gone fishing", and went to the London Library. In the reading room there was a Who's Who in Broadcasting. GLJ is forty-nine. Educated Haileybury. Went into family newspaper business. Sold it out and became theatre impresario. Moved from this to film industry. List of credits as director or producer. Married three times. One son and one daughter from first marriage. Hobbies: flying, golf and collecting military memorabilia. No clubs listed and address given as care of Humberside TV.

'I came back to the office. Incidentally, I didn't really hang up a notice saying "Gone fishing". Thought I'd better tell you now or you'd have another sleepless night and I might not get my pressie. I phoned Humberside and got through to Jackson's secretary. I said I was on the admin staff at Sunningdale. I apologised profusely and said we'd mislaid a list of acceptances for a gala dinner following a celebrity Pro-Am tournament. Did Mr Jackson have a booking for the sixth of September at Sunningdale? She looked at his diary and said no he hadn't. I asked her to double-check as someone here was sure he'd accepted. "I'm sure," she said; "as a matter of fact he's playing golf at his own club on that day." "What club is that?" I asked innocently. "The Swanley Bar," she said.

'Next I took advantage of that massive sub you pay just to be a customer of Infofile. They reckon to have lists of members of every respectable club and some disreputable ones too. I keyed in the code and asked if there was a register of members of golf clubs. The answer was "Affirmative for the following clubs" and a list came on the screen. It rolled over and eventually Swanley Bar came up. I asked for a full list of members. After a pause it came up, rolling slowly. And there was Jackson's name and private address. And what else, do you think? Wait for it. T J Marler. How about that! But his address was given in St Martins, Guernsey. This didn't seem right to me. Usually clubs have a residential qualification with a limited radius of the golf course. I asked for verification. It was verified. So then I checked on Infofile's other registers. Apart from banking with the Midland he seems to have slipped through their net.

122

'I decided to call it a day on high-tech and went back to humdrum old-fashioned enquiries. On the common old telephone I called up the Guernsey number given as Marler's number on the Swanley Bar list. A woman answered. I did the market research line and asked to speak to Mr Marler. She said, "He doesn't live here any more," and slammed down the phone. I toyed with the idea of doing the same on Jackson's private number but decided not to. You might have disapproved. That's typical of me. Always trying to anticipate your reactions. One day you're going to enter me for one of those perfect secretary competitions. Yes? That's all. See you.'

'Good girl,' said Samson aloud.

It had been a long day and tomorrow might be equally long. He poured himself a nightcap whisky, a favourite malt which he drank when he wanted to treat himself to a celebratory drink. He felt like celebrating. Pieces in the puzzle set by Pensom were slotting into place.

After a sparse breakfast he left for the office. He wanted to arrive before Shandy so that he could put a small parcel on her desk. It contained a bottle of *Mystère* by Rochas which he'd bought at the duty-free shop at Strasbourg. He didn't know whether she liked the scent but he liked its name and, more important, it wasn't cheap.

He was in his room when she arrived. He heard a little squeal of delight and she burst into his room. 'You did remember me!'

She was round his desk and kissing his cheek before he could move, and when he did move it was a wriggle of embarrassment. He wasn't used to affectionate gestures and never knew quite how to cope on the rare occasions when someone was demonstrative.

'It's nothing,' he muttered.

'It isn't nothing. And how did you know I'd switched to *Mystère*?'

With Shandy he always, or almost always, spoke the

123

truth. 'I didn't know.'

'An inspired guess?'

'Maybe.' He switched the conversation to a less personal level. 'Anything crop up yesterday?'

'I booked an appointment for you to check security at Wendlehurst's and I got the pathologist's report in the Amhurst case. I don't believe Mrs Amhurst has a leg to stand on. The hospital did everything humanly possible. Oh yes, and Pensom called. It was quite late. I'd been working late, believe it or not. The jaunt to the London Library put me back. I was just packing up when his call came through. It was after I'd spoken on the answerphone and thought it could wait till this morning.'

'What did he want?'

'He wanted to speak to you. I said you'd gone to Scotland.'

'How did he react?'

'He said, "Oh, God." I asked if anything was wrong. He said no and then changed it to yes, and havered and hovered, and then he said, "I'll be all right," but he didn't sound very confident, and he finished by asking if you'd get in touch as soon as you got back. I asked if he'd be on the same phone number, or where we should contact him. He gave a funny laugh and said, "I'll be here. I'm not moving out."'

'He said he wasn't moving out?'

A defensive expression came to Shandy's face on having her own words thrown back as a question. 'That's what he said.'

'Did he sound frightened? Threatened? Or did it sound as if he wanted to stay in because he wasn't feeling well. A summer chill, maybe.'

'He sounded a bit nervy. On edge.'

'Would you give him a call and ask if he'd like to come here this morning?'

'Right.' She left the room.

Samson walked over to the window and looked out. The street was alive with late office workers hurrying from the railway station and early shoppers making their way to and from the supermarket at the end of the street. About thirty yards down the street a car stopped on double yellow lines and two men jumped out. The car drove off. The men made for the building opposite and let themselves in with a key.

He was about to return to his desk when he spotted movement near the window on the first floor of the building opposite. He ducked out of sight and then peered round the curtains to see the two men looking directly towards him. Were they prospective lessees or had the man he roughed up in the multi-storey car park managed to follow him and find out where he worked? If so, he was under surveillance visually and with the rapid advances in the development of electronic eavesdropping he might soon be having his conversations taped. For a moment he considered drawing the curtains but this would only inform the watchers that he knew he was under observation.

He went to Shandy's room and told her of this new development.

'I've already fixed an appointment for Pensom at eleven,' she said.

'Get him again, will you? I'll take it in here.'

When he was connected Samson said, 'John Samson here. A slight change of plan.'

'I want to see you urgently.' The voice came through in a whisper as though Pensom wanted to avoid being overheard.

'And so you shall, but at your place.'

A pause. 'Here? Why?'

'Don't worry, there'll be no extra cost.'

'But my friend lives here.'

'We'll meet somewhere outside then.'

'No, wait. I can cook up a story. You come here. I'll see you in my room. When can I expect you?'

'The morning mail hasn't arrived yet but it's due. I'll be along as soon as I've checked through it. Incidentally, your whereabouts haven't been discovered, have they?'

'Not as far as I know, but that's what's worrying me.' His voice became almost inaudible. 'My friend Anthony did something stupid yesterday while you were in Scotland. I'll tell you about it. I must go now. Goodbye.'

After dealing with the morning mail Samson said, 'I'm off now. Expect me when you see me. I'm leaving by the fire escape at the back but I may come in at the front when I've seen Pensom, but don't worry if you hear noises at the back.'

She gave him a long look.

'What is it?' he asked.

'You will take care, won't you?'

His eyes crinkled at the corners. 'I'm not in any danger.'

'I hope not, but I've got the funniest feeling about this case. It could end in tragedy.'

'Woman's intuition,' he chuckled.

She tossed back her head. 'All right. Don't take care. See if I care.' Her face puckered and she looked quickly away.

'See you,' he said.

She made no reply.

As he walked down the metal steps of the fire escape Samson wished the parting from Shandy had been better, but by the time he reached an alley leading to a back street his thoughts were concentrated on the meeting ahead. Pensom had some questions to answer.

SOME PREDATORS ARE MALE
Part 5

Anthony Vestier had spent most of his professional life playing small parts in repertory but towards the end of his career he appeared in films typecast as an elderly English eccentric. It was debatable whether he was naturally an elderly eccentric and therefore simply playing himself or whether he had become an elderly eccentric through identifying too closely with the role. He was arthritic and walked everywhere with the aid of a stick. Thinning grey locks rested on the collar of a bottle-green velvet jacket which he wore all the year round together with a droopy black tie. 'It's in mourning for the death of a fine actor,' he would reply to anyone who mentioned the tie. If the enquiry, 'Which actor?' was made, he'd answer, 'Me. No one will mourn me when I'm dead so I might as well mourn myself now.' Depending on whether he was in a manic or depressive phase he would laugh at his joke or squeeze tears into his eyes. He was seventy-three years old.

He had a thousand acquaintances and a few friends. Neil Pensom ranked as a friend because he made sure Anthony was never alone at Christmas, the anniversary of the death of Anthony's thirty-year companion and lover, a butcher from Lambeth. Anthony had fallen in love with him while watching his hands as he dextrously filleted joints of meat. Now retired, Anthony was painfully typing with crabbed fingers an autobiography tentatively titled, *Reminiscences of an Old Actor*. Those who had read extracts were unanimous in agreeing that no publisher in his right mind would accept the book for publication, but they never told Anthony as much in case it sent him plummeting into a depressive phase. His phases switched from plus to minus or minus to plus as rapidly as the switch on an electrical circuit; the arrival of Neil Pensom at his flat operated the switch and his mental outlook hit a bright high.

'Neil, my dear fellow. What are you doing here? Lovely to see you. It's not babe-in-a-manger day yet, is it?'

'I wondered if you could put me up for a while. My place is uninhabitable. I'm having alterations done.'

'Installing a crib for the anticipated happy event?'

'The kitchen is being redesigned and my bedroom redecorated.'

'How traumatic. Of course you shall stay. And for as long as you like. Until the Virgin has had her annual delivery if you wish.'

'Just a few days. It's very kind of you.'

'Always room at this inn, dear boy, if you don't mind the chaos.'

Pensom cleared an armchair of a job lot of books, a pile of 78 records, and the cylinder head from an old Austin Ascot 12.4, and sat down. Anthony made a pot of tea from tea bags stored in a brass thurible. He had once been a devout Anglo-Catholic and some of the debris in his flat were mementoes. When the tea was ready he said, 'Now tell me all. What's the colour motif in your bedroom to be?'

'Pale greens and browns.'

'Non-stimulating colours. Sensible if not very adventurous.'

'What about you? Still working on the book?'

'The only memorial of my days. Not that I give a fig for posterity, the harlot. No, it's all temporal vanity and I suppose I shall have to find a vanity publisher if I can raise the wind.'

Pensom looked for somewhere to rest a mug of tea. There was no available space and so he placed it carefully by his feet on a threadbare carpet. While engaged in this manoeuvre he said, 'I'd like to borrow your typewriter when you're not using it.'

'With the greatest pleasure. Crafty letters to creditors or something more creative?'

'I've got an idea for a story. It could make a TV play.'

'Marvellous!' Anthony Vestier clapped his hands and winced with pain. 'What's the storyline?'

'It's about a man remorselessly pursued by a woman who's taken a fancy to him but he doesn't want to know.'

'A universal theme. I have a story like that in my book. She saw me when I was playing *French without Tears* at Richmond. Followed me everywhere and would have swallowed me alive given half a chance. Dear Clive saw her off in the end. Is yours a comedy?'

'Sort of.' Pensom gingerly lifted his mug of tea and took a sip. 'Actually, more like a black farce.'

Anthony reached for his stick and used it to retrieve a packet of cigarettes lying on the floor. With an effort he picked up the packet and lighted a cigarette.

Pensom got to his feet. 'Let me find you an ashtray.'

'No need, dear boy. Ash does the carpet good. There's a line in *George and Margaret*. You know the one? Goes, "That's a lazy habit invented by a lazy man and it's been a boon to all lazy men ever since," or something like.' He broke into a fit of coughing and his eyes watered. 'It's me tubes,' he wheezed. 'By the way, the spare room isn't any too tidy. Stuff piled on the bed.'

'Don't worry about that. I'll shift it. Incidentally, I shall insist on contributing to household expenses.'

Anthony waved his stick. 'Wouldn't hear of it. Not unless your boat's come home or you've pulled off the big one at last.'

Pensom gave a wry smile. 'No such luck, but I've managed a bit more on overdraft.'

'Maybe your play will earn a few coppers.'

Pensom didn't want to talk about his 'play'. Anthony wasn't discreet. He'd talk about anything and everything to anyone who'd care to listen. 'A few coppers is about all it will earn, I expect. If it's all right I'll take a look at the spare room now. Start clearing the stuff from the bed and clear a space for the typewriter.'

'I can't offer to give a hand. I'd be more hindrance than help. Just dump things wherever you like. It won't make any difference overall.'

During the next two days Pensom worked on his account and if quoted conversations weren't accurate in every respect he was sure the contents and gist were correct as were all incidental observations. He had hoped by putting everything down he might arrive at a solution but when this seemed unlikely he realised that, as anticipated, he would certainly need some professional help in discovering who was subjecting him to pointless oppression.

It wasn't easy to work in an environment of total disorder. Relics of a theatrical life, old props, programmes and photographs, were scattered among brass and copper ornaments which Anthony had inherited from an aunt. There were three panels of stained glass, some butcher's implements including a huge cleaver and an iron anvil. Pensom perched on a bar-stool in front of a small tripod table and pecked out his story on an ancient portable Remington. From time to time he was interrupted by Anthony, who had become intensely curious about the progress of the TV play and would ask about the possibilities of Humberside TV taking it. 'Damn it all, man, you should try it with them first. They won't take it kindly if you sell elsewhere.'

Pensom began to wish he'd thought up a different cover story. As a break he would go out and wander around Battersea Gardens and shop for food and other necessaries. It was after an afternoon expedition on the second day that he caught Anthony reading the typescript.

'Good stuff this, old chap. Could do with more touches of humour though. And some of the lines aren't good for an actor. You need to sharpen up the dialogue. But why on earth write it like a novel? Why not write it as a script?'

'I didn't give you permission.'

'I know, I *know*.' When caught at a disadvantage Anthony adopted the old trick of repeating brief statements twice with heavy emphasis on the final word. Years of saying, 'You are . . . You *are*!' had left an indelible mark.

'I'm not like you,' said Pensom, containing the anger he felt, 'I don't like people to read my "work in progress".'

'Sorry. Won't do it again.' The old man's eyes gleamed mischievously. 'At any rate, I'll try not to get caught again. By the way, you'll find pencil notes in the margin. I know a spot of German. Made one or two corrections and put in the proper Schiller quotation which doesn't mention love although love is the illusion he means.'

Pensom grabbed the typescript and went to his room. There wasn't much left to write and as he slipped paper into the Remington he decided to hire a private detective in the morning. He liked Anthony well enough but the prevailing disorder and constant interruptions irritated him.

By seven in the evening he had finished the narrative. He stapled the top copy and put the carbon copy in a folder. For at least the tenth time that day Anthony poked his head round the door.

'Care for a pizza and green salad, old chap?'

'That would be fine.'

'I'll start cooking then.'

The door closed. Being called 'old chap', 'dear boy' and 'old fellow' was another annoyance, but he'd have to stick it out a few more days. While Anthony was in the kitchen he looked up 'Detective Agencies' in Yellow Pages. The larger organisations claimed expertise in electronic surveillance, de-bugging and security consultancy. Pensom favoured smaller firms which he thought would give more personal attention to his problem. In the end he narrowed down the field to three possibilities. He closed his eyes and stabbed the page with a pin. The winner, nearest to the pin, was John Samson whose advertisment read: 'Every sort of private investigation undertaken with utmost discretion and in complete confidence, at home or abroad.'

After the meal, and having watched the newscast on television, he went to bed. Here he was spared Anthony's endless reminiscences and could yet again try to understand why he had been selected as the butt of some bad-taste joke or as the target for something more sinister.

The following day, on a morning which promised to be a continuance of the heatwave, he left Anthony's apartment intending to telephone John Samson from a call-box but after trying three boxes and finding all had been vandalised he took a cab and went to the detective without an appointment.

Three children were kicking a ball around outside the apartment block and a man in overalls was cleaning ground floor windows. Samson decided to check that the man was a genuine cleaner and not someone waiting and watching for Pensom. 'Do you sell honey?' he asked.

The cleaner turned round. 'You talking to me?'

'Yes. Do you sell honey?'

With a ceremonious and deliberate gesture the cleaner draped a chamois leather over a bucket and squared up to Samson. 'You trying to be funny?'

'No. I'm asking if you sell honey.'

'Piss off,' said the window cleaner, 'or I'll land one on you.'

Samson knew instinctively this was not a loiterer intent on watching for his client.

'My mistake,' he said. He pressed a button next to

134

number nine on the list of occupants.

A voice said, 'Hello. Who's that?'

'John Samson.'

'Come up, Mr Samson. I'll open the door. The lift is on the left. Number nine is on the second floor. Or you can come up the staircase.'

A minute later, seated in the chaos of Pensom's room, he said, 'Now tell me. What did you mean when you said your friend did something stupid yesterday?'

'You've read my story?'

'Yes.'

Pensom perched himself on the bar-stool. 'You believe it, I hope.'

'Why not?'

Pensom jerked his thumb in the direction of the sitting room. 'He thinks it's the basis of a TV script. And he's done something which could spoil this as a safe hideaway.' Pensom rubbed his brow. He looked weary and his dark brown blazer and fawn slacks looked tired too. 'I'd better begin at the beginning. The day before I came to see you I stupidly left a carbon copy in my room. Anthony went in and read it. Everything except the last two pages. I was pretty angry. Then yesterday, when you were in Scotland, I paid a visit to my mother's grave. She's buried in Cheltenham. The visit took the best part of a day. While I was away, Anthony, thinking he was doing me a good turn, did something he hardly ever does these days. It's too painful. But he managed to hobble down to the Feathers, his local pub, in the hope of seeing a regular there who's connected with the book publishing business. I think the guy reads for a publisher. Anyway, he took the carbon copy and showed it to this man.' Pensom paused to light a cigarette. 'I'd given these up,' he said, exhaling a thin plume of smoke, 'but I've started again.'

'Excuse my asking,' said Samson, 'but what's a blacksmith's anvil doing in here?'

Pensom relaxed slightly and gave a faint smile. 'It's Anthony's. He was in some village in the Midlands, he was playing at the nearby town, and I don't know how it came about but he met a carpenter. I think it was in a butcher's shop. Anthony haunted butcher's shops at one time. Anyway, he got talking to the carpenter and discovered he made coffins for an undertaker. Anthony had always wanted a coffin of his own and he went back to this guy's workshop which was once a forge. He saw the anvil and bid for it and bought it. Don't ask me why. Perhaps he was going through his Wagner phase.'

'And didn't get the coffin?' asked Samson, his curiosity aroused.

'Oh, yes. It's in his bedroom here. Now he's so infirm he hardly ever lies in it, but at one time he used to sleep in it.'

Samson would like to have continued the conversation but knew he ought to continue with business. First, however, he decided to change seats. The chair he'd been given was an antique sewing chair with its seat close to the floor. 'I think I'd sooner sit on that,' he said, indicating the anvil.

'Sure. I'll get you a cushion.'

'No need.' Samson patted his backside. 'I carry my own cushion around with me.' He went and sat on the anvil. 'That's better. What happened when your friend showed your story to the publishing man?'

'I gather the guy sampled bits here and there and said it wasn't bad but too short for anything commercial. He suggested I should lengthen it. When I got back from Cheltenham Anthony told me what he'd done. He was pleased with himself. He thought he'd done me a good turn and what the reader had said would encourage me to finish the story. I was livid. This is a private matter. I don't want the world to know someone's fooling around with my life. And I don't want anyone to find me.'

'Tell me about Marler,' said Samson.

136

Pensom shifted on the stool. 'He's a creditor.'

'How much do you owe him?'

'A few hundred. Maybe a bit more.'

Samson guessed the sum was much more.

'But there'd be no point in him prosecuting me,' Pensom continued. 'It would be self-defeating.'

'Why do you say "prosecuting"?'

'Did I? I meant persecuting. A slip of the tongue.'

'Why does Marler hate the sight of blood?'

'I don't know.'

'You wrote that he did.'

'I think I heard it somewhere.'

'You wrote that he hated the sight of blood, but you don't know where you got the information from. How much else in your story is hearsay?'

'None of it,' said Pensom indignantly.

'You also wrote that when the lights in the juggernaut were dimmed for the film show you wondered if it was so that you could take advantage of the poor light to start a fight. But you stated you didn't like this sort of physical contact, with reason. What did you mean, "with reason"?'

'What is this?' Pensom burst out. 'Are you trying to harass me? Are you one of them?'

Samson smiled compassionately. If he'd been wearing a dog-collar he could have passed for a sympathetic priest exercising loving patience with a troubled sinner.

'I'm on your side. I'm trying to help. But you have to help me. I don't think you've told me everything. I think you're holding something back. I'm trying to find out what it is.'

'What do you want? My whole life story?'

'I want to know why you dislike physical contact.' Samson paused to give emphasis to his next statement. 'You don't like the idea of fighting. Marler doesn't like the sight of blood. You have a sort of squeamishness in common, haven't you?'

137

Pensom jumped to his feet and began striding up and down the room using the one strip of carpet that was uncluttered. Samson sat calmly on the anvil, waiting. At last Pensom stopped pacing. 'All right. I'll tell you. But it doesn't have any bearing.'

'Let me judge that.'

'I got hooked on gambling when I was fourteen. I would steal from my mother's purse to go to the amusement arcade. Only a few pennies, and not every day. Later, I graduated to gaming clubs and casinos. When I was about twenty I happened to go into an arcade near Piccadilly Circus. It was fairly full, mostly of men and youngsters. I struck up a conversation with a guy of about my age. He'd used all his money and was just watching. To cut a long story short, I discovered he hadn't eaten and, as I was hungry, I thought I'd treat him to a meal. Then I found he had nowhere to go that night. It was bitterly cold. On the spur of the moment I invited him home. Mother was in hospital and I had the house to myself.' Pensom paused and looked Samson straight in the eyes. 'That's all there was to it as far as I was concerned.' He gave a bitter laugh. 'I thought I was being a good Samaritan.'

'I made up a bed for him in the spare room and went to bed in my own room. I soon fell asleep. I was tired. I was woken in the middle of the night by him. He was in my bed . . . and touching me. I went berserk. I threw him out of bed, switched on the light and gave him a beating. I hit him hard. By the time I cooled down there was blood all over the place. On his face and my pyjamas. He was lying on the floor, out cold. I panicked. I thought I'd killed him. But he recovered. I helped him to his feet. He stared at the blood on my pyjamas and went into a dead faint. He passed out two or three times as I drove him to the casualty department of the nearest hospital. He needed medical attention. I was fairly sure I'd broken his nose. I rushed him to the hospital entrance and then made my getaway. I vowed then never to get into a fight again.'

Pensom stopped abruptly. He looked exhausted.

'And that's how you met Marler?' Samson asked.

'Yes.'

'Did you keep in touch with him?'

'No, but he kept the tabs on me. He made money, I don't know how, but I can guess. I learned later he set himself up in a small way with a basement club where they played blackjack and poker. From then on he prospered. But I didn't know about this. I'd virtually forgotten him, but he hadn't forgotten me. I didn't suspect anything when I was given credit well over the limit at a certain club. I thought it was because I'd let it be known that Mother was well-off and I'd inherit one day. And the credit kept on being given. And I kept on writing IOUs. When I was more than ten thousand down, a guy called on me. His boss, Mr Marler, had sent him to collect. I was given a week to find the money.' Pensom's voice sank to a whisper. 'I was beside myself with worry.'

Although he was facing Samson his eyes seemed inner directed and there was pain in what he saw in his mind.

'I should have gone to the police but I was in a state of total confusion. I couldn't bear the thought of a grilling and maybe a court case. Mother was dying and I had this terrible pressure put on me. But I thought I'd soon be comfortably off. I pleaded for time and was given a month. During that time Mother died. And then came the big shock. Unknown to me Mother had changed her will. I only get a life interest on income from the capital. When I die the capital is divided between three charities. Her solicitor told me it was to protect me against myself. He said if I contested the will he'd have to appear against me as the lawyer representing the charities. And that's the present position. I haven't had any further visits from one of Marler's toughs but I dread one day someone will corner me and ask for the money. Marler still has the IOUs.

139

Needless to say, I tried to raise the wind by gambling, but without luck ... And now you know the full story, Mr Samson.'

Samson allowed him a few moments to recover and then said, 'Was total confusion the only reason you didn't go to the police?'

'No, my career was at stake. I've had the feeling for some time that Humberside have wanted to get rid of me. More so since Mother's death. I haven't been a hundred per cent. But I've always done what's been asked of me. If it became public that I had gambling debts I'd be fired, and I'd have a job convincing an industrial tribunal it was unfair dismissal. That's another reason why I haven't been to the police.' Pensom gave an anguished look. 'Do you think I should go?'

Samson regarded his client with genuine compassion. It sometimes happened that a man or woman would come to him with a problem and present it in a way of their own choosing, sometimes offhand, sometimes arrogantly; but before the end of the case they would be submissively asking advice. The change in attitude didn't give him a sense of power so much as a sense of pity. In his view most men and women always desired more than they could ever achieve and were incapable of accepting that simply to exist all their lives on the same plateau, without moving downwards, is an achievement in itself.

'I wouldn't recommend going to the police. Not at this stage anyway.'

'What do you recommend?'

'What sort of relationship do you have with Geraint Lloyd Jackson?'

'Not bad. We get along. His wife might not like me but that's different.'

'Why shouldn't she like you?'

'No reason except I don't flirt with her. GLJ has the knack of marrying the same type of woman every time he gets hitched. Repetition compulsion I think it's called. He likes open marriage and picks women with the same inclinations.'

Samson surreptitiously glanced at his watch. His metabolism was habituated to a mid-morning snack and he was beginning to feel hungry. He wished he had eaten a better breakfast.

Pensom had momentarily been lost in thought. He started speaking again. 'It was at the end of the shooting of *Maverick Mosquito*. We had the usual party and Jill, GLJ's latest wife, more or less threw herself at me. Quite openly. He didn't seem to mind. But maybe he did, after all.' Pensom gave Samson a curious look. 'You don't think GLJ is mixed up in all this, do you?'

'Yes.'

Pensom leaned forward. 'How? Why?'

'How is easy to answer. Everywhere you went there were opportunities to film you. As for why, I've got a theory.'

'Yes?'

'Does GLJ have affairs on the side?'

Pensom hesitated before replying. 'I don't know for sure, but I think so. Rumour has it that he's got a mews flat in Mayfair. He's been seen in the Hilton with a woman. She was described as petite. All GLJ's wives have been petite, fluttery, feminine. He rather likes playing the macho bit.'

'Would you describe Gerda Vogel as petite, fluttery and feminine?'

Pensom's fatigue had vanished. 'You don't think . . .'

'I didn't go to Scotland,' said Samson. 'I went to Germany.' Hurriedly he added, 'At my expense. It was an extended private visit to Strasbourg.'

He then told of his visit to the cemetery where there was no hut, called at the Vogels to find no one at home, and by chance met Eva Grunblatt.

'I made out I was a friend of the Vogels and was very disappointed to have missed them. It was a hot day; she

141

invited me in for a drink. I discovered she was a part-time actress. She showed me an album of cuttings and photos. There was a big glossy photo of her playing the part of an ugly step-sister in Cinderella. She was heavily made up and had a large hairy mole on her cheek.'

Samson paused to allow the information to sink in.

'My God! Not Amanda?'

'I'd guess so.'

Pensom said, 'I'm amazed. So she doesn't really have a mole with black hairs?'

'No.'

'I'm amazed,' said Pensom again.

Samson waited for the amazement to dissipate. One of the rewards of his job was the fleeting pleasure of surprising a client with unexpected information.

'She was no fool,' he went on. 'Before I left she'd become suspicious. There was someone waiting for me with a camera when I got back to Heathrow. They know I'm involved, but they've lost you. That's why I came here.'

'You may have been followed today.'

'No. I made sure I wasn't.'

'What about the Vogels? They're mixed up in this?'

'They must be,' said Samson.

'The woman who was seen at the Hilton with GLJ could have been Gerda.'

'It probably was. Eva Grunblatt let it slip that when the Vogels came over here together Hans would go off with a party of schoolboys while Gerda stayed in London where she could meet someone flamboyant, a character, someone in television.'

Pensom shook his head. 'I can't understand it. She seemed to worship Hans. And I liked him even though he inflicted Amanda on me . . . What now, Mr Samson?'

'There are quite a few people involved. There's GLJ, a director. There are three known in acting parts – Frau Grunblatt and the Vogels. Other actors, or participators, are the men who abducted you and the woman in your flat. The men may have been German and speaking a dialect you didn't recognise. I know that GLJ has contacts with TV companies abroad. I also believe he knows Marler. They belong to the same golf club. So Marler may be in it too.'

'Marler?'

'Are his initials TJ?'

'They may be. I knew him as Julian.' Pensom gave a hollow laugh as if refuge in humour was the best way of confronting something he didn't understand. 'The same golf club? It's incredible. I'd never have dreamed golf was his scene. And how on earth does he think he'll get money out of me by setting me up as some sort of target for sick jokes?'

'You said there haven't been any demands recently?'

'That's right.'

'I wonder,' Samson began, and then broke off what he was going to say.

'Maybe he's getting revenge for that time I hit him,' said Pensom. 'Trying to drive me mad. No, I can't buy that.'

'Tell me something. This production you were engaged on – the one about diamond smuggling. You were sent to Antwerp to look out for locations. Did you see the script for the play?'

'No. That was a bit unusual. I was only given a three-page synopsis.'

'Normally you'd expect to see a script before you went looking for locations?'

'Normally, yes.'

'No money wasted on a script,' Samson mused. 'What about casting?'

'GLJ had one or two fairly big names in mind.' Pensom paused and his eyes became momentarily blank. Then, 'Now I come to think of it GLJ told me not to talk around about the assignation. Something about copyright and loose ends needing to be tidied up.' As he spoke he became more animated. 'That's right, I remember now, he reckoned Anglia might pip us if they got wind of the project.'

'So very few people in Humberside could have known about it?'

'Very few. What are you leading up to?'

'I don't think there was ever any intention to make a film about diamond smuggling. It was a pretext to get you to go to places where you could yourself be filmed.'

Pensom considered the proposition. 'I can see that. But for what purpose?'

'I don't watch much television,' replied Samson, 'but I do know there are programmes in Britain and America, and elsewhere for all I know, where individuals are duped into playing a ridiculous role in front of hidden cameras. They have no idea the thing is being staged and their reactions are recorded. You know the programmes I mean?'

'Sure. Candid Camera is one.'

'Are these programmes popular?'

'Fairly popular. Audiences enjoy watching other people being taken for a ride.'

Samson nodded. 'The misfortunes of others have always been a popular spectacle. Let's suppose in your case that instead of the usual three or four minutes someone has the idea of making a full-length film. You are sent on what you think is a *bona fide* mission but we, the audience, know you're going to encounter all sorts of unusual situations. As each new scene unfolds your bewilderment and discomfiture are recorded. An amused voice-over could link each episode.' He looked at Pensom. 'Is that beyond belief?'

'Not beyond belief, but far-fetched.'

'Why?'

'For one thing, whoever is the central character must know eventually what's happened. He could sue.'

'If he's got legal grounds, maybe.'

'I know what you're getting at, Mr Samson, but it's hard to believe . . . I mean, the expense . . . organisation. The secrecy. Do you really think I've been set up for a Candid Camera-type film?'

'You'd be an ideal candidate. You live alone. You have no close relatives. No wife and, so far as I know, no girlfriend. Nobody is going to miss you if you disappear for a few days. Your pay-off for being the film's fall-guy could be the return of the IOUs. Something like this might have been hatched up at the nineteenth hole. You haven't found it funny, but Marler and GLJ may have split their sides.'

Pensom said nothing.

'You may think it far-fetched,' Samson continued, 'but it's the only theory I've got at the moment.'

Pensom gazed into space as he tried to assimilate the implications. When he spoke his voice was husky. 'I couldn't bear it. To have audiences laughing . . . Be a butt . . .'

'But if the terms were financially acceptable?'

'It'd be marvellous to have Marler off my back but how could I carry on with my job? And there would be publicity. I'd hate that. Isn't there some way it could be stopped? That is, if you're right.'

Samson eased himself off the anvil and stretched his legs. 'I've thought about that. It struck me you might have a case for libel. I had a look at my law books during the night – I don't sleep too well – and I discovered it's possible to libel on film as well as in written material. And if someone is exposed to ridicule on film there might be a basis for a libel action. You'd have to take expert legal advice on that. But if you accept payment for any part in the film you'd naturally have no case at all. Another remedy would be to get an injunction to prevent showing of the film, but you'd have to prove a film was being made, and we haven't got to that stage. Anyway, I daresay any action you took would be contested.'

145

'It'd be contested all right, by fair means or foul. Marler's got a reputation for being ruthless.' The colour faded from Pensom's cheeks. 'I've just had a thought. Suppose when they've got all the film they want – whoever *they* are – they decide to get rid of me. For good. There wouldn't be any libel case or anything else.'

'Come on now. It's not as bad as all that. Don't get things out of proportion. This is mostly guesswork.'

'Mr Samson, the fact that I've been stuck in intolerable situations, and filmed in them, isn't guesswork any more, so far as I'm concerned. The only guesswork is how it's all going to end.'

Samson went back to the anvil and this time straddled it as though riding an iron hobby-horse. 'We have the advantage, the initiative,' he said. 'I think my office is being watched, but the watchers don't know I know, and this gives me an edge. They have no idea where you are, and this gives you an edge. It needn't concern us whether the film is being made for public or private consumption. But if they have other episodes planned your disappearance will concern them. I doubt if scenes in Antwerp, the juggernaut, the Vogels' house and your flat are enough. No, we'll have to use our advantage.'

'What's the next move then?' asked Pensom.

'Anvils weren't made to be sat upon,' said Samson, 'my next move is off this one.' He stood up. 'Can I use the side of your bed?'

'Of course.'

'On second thoughts, perhaps not. We might as well go.'

'Go? Where?' Pensom looked and sounded startled.

'To your flat. I want to see how Felicity Flowerdew copes with me.'

A flicker of anxiety crossed Pensom's face. 'You think it's safe?'

'Nothing is safe. There's no such thing as absolute security, any more than there is absolute liberty, equality

146

or fraternity. All hopeless ideals. I want you to leave ahead of me. I'll follow, and when I'm sure there's no tail on either of us I'll catch up with you. If I don't, get back here as fast as you can. But if everything's all right, and I catch up with you, we'll go to the nearest Post Office. I want to put a call through to my secretary. Then we'll take a taxi to your flat.'

'I won't tell Anthony where we're going.'

'Don't. In variation poker he'd be a wild card.'

Pensom smiled. 'He's a card in real life.'

'Shandy?'

'Yes?'

'What's the weather like in Hong Kong?'

'I'll find out.'

'Good. Ring me back on o-nine-o, eight-seven-six-two.'

On the rare occasions when Samson suspected his phone might be tapped he would ask about the weather in Hong Kong. Shandy would then hurry upstairs to the flat above their office where an elderly woman earned a meagre living from embroidering tablecloths. Samson paid her telephone rental on the understanding that he could use her phone at any time.

He waited in the call-box and soon Shandy's call came through.

'I want you to get in touch with the estate agents who are handling the sale of the place opposite. Tell them you've seen someone there and wonder if it's in order. Do they have authority to be on the premises? If they do, try to find out who they are.'

'Will do. How's it going?'

'Not bad. I'm just off to Dulwich with our client to make the acquaintance of Miss Flowerdew.'

'Good luck.'

'I think you might have been right to warn me to take care. Sorry I mocked your intuition.'

A light laugh came down the line. 'You're making your peace with me in case the worst happens. You're forgiven. And do take care.'

'I will. See you.'

In the taxi Samson asked who held the deeds of Pensom's flat.

'The Halifax Building Society. I had to get a mortgage. And my bank has a second mortgage.'

'A solicitor acted for you in the transaction?'

'Yes. But not the guy who handled Mother's estate. I fell out with him.'

'So you've plenty of evidence that it's yours. The title will be registered with the Land Registry together with notice of the mortgages.'

They were seated side by side in the back of a sedan which was the legitimate successor of the sedan-chair, a black London taxi. A notice on the partition window requested passengers not to smoke. As the taxi drifted to a halt at traffic lights Samson said, 'Didn't you think of going back and having it out with the fair Felicity before you came to see me?'

'The idea crossed my mind, but the thought that Amanda might still be there . . .'

'You could have gone to your solicitor.'

'I thought of that, and the police, but in the end I decided this was the best way. Marler's tentacles spread wide, and there are bent lawyers and bent coppers.' Pensom sighed. 'When you're in my position you get very cautious.'

'From what you wrote,' said Samson, 'I thought you'd ruled out Marler. It would be counter-productive for him to put you through the mill.'

'That's right. I did think that. But then again, I had doubts. I was very confused.'

The taxi moved off and within minutes they were driving

148

past a sports ground. 'We're getting close,' said Pensom.

'It's a more salubrious area than mine. What made you decide to live here?'

'Oh, it's a long story. . . . Do you think Amanda – I mean, Eva Grunblatt – will still be there?'

'Not unless she's flown in from Germany since I saw her yesterday.'

Pensom gave a nervous laugh. 'I must pull myself together. I shouldn't be afraid of a woman. But there's something about her.' He searched for an exact description. 'In a way she possesses a fearful fascination. The sort a stoat has over a rabbit. Not that I'm a rabbit,' he added quickly.

'Most men are basically afraid of women,' remarked Samson, 'although few would admit it. The history of western civilisation might have been quite different if St Paul hadn't been afraid of women. But this isn't the time or place to argue about that. Is there a tradesman's entrance at the back of your block of flats?'

'Yes.'

'Tell the driver how to get there. It's unlikely there'll be a watch on the place but if there is it would be at the front.'

Pensom tapped the dividing panel and the driver slid it back.

'If you turn right at the next road you'll have a short cut to the address. It'll take you to the back entrance.'

'I got you, *Señor*.'

The taxi moved over to the crown of the road. Soon it pulled up in a bay at the rear of the block. Samson gave the driver a ten-pound note and asked him to wait.

At the back door Pensom inserted a key. He turned it and the door opened. 'You see,' he said, 'this lock hasn't been tampered with.' He held up another key. 'But this one doesn't fit my own lock any more.'

When they stepped out of the elevator and on to the landing Pensom said, 'I'll show you what I mean about my

149

key, or were you intending to ring the bell?'

'Try the key,' said Samson. 'I'll ring the bell at the same time. She won't hear the sound of the key.'

Pensom stopped in front of a door numbered fourteen. As he inserted the key, Samson pressed the bell-push. No one answered the bell but the lock responded to Pensom's key and with a light push the door swung open.

The two men looked at each other.

'I don't understand it,' said Pensom. His feet didn't move but his body swayed; it was as if his shoes were affixed to the floor by Superglue.

Samson side-stepped to avoid him. 'She's either gone out or she's in her bath,' he said. And then, because Pensom looked as though he'd seen a ghost, 'What is it?'

Pensom walked forward unsteadily. 'It's incredible. Everything's back to normal.' He turned to Samson. 'Everything's been replaced.'

'Has it?' said Samson and the words sounded like ironic comment rather than a polite query; it was the sound of mistrust. He was in a quandary. Either Felicity Flowerdew had left, and props men had restored the flat to its original state, or Pensom had been telling a string of lies and the flat had never been disturbed by Felicity Flowerdew or anyone else.

'I can't believe it,' said Pensom. He hurried to the main bedroom. It was unlocked and except for a crookedly hung picture exactly as it had been when he last occupied it.

Samson was close behind. 'Nothing missing, Mr Pensom?'

'Not that I can see.'

'Nothing changed?'

Pensom returned to the living room. 'Some ornaments are a bit out of place but everything's been put back.'

'So you say.'

Pensom swung round. 'What do you mean?'

'I'm not sure whether you're the victim of a perverted

150

sense of humour or you're in urgent need of the services of a psychiatrist, but I'm going to find out. And if you've been taking me for a ride, Mr Pensom, it will be an expensive one for you. That's a binding promise.'

Pensom's hands went up to cover his face. 'How much more do I have to take? I've been completely honest with you.'

Samson didn't waste time in answering. If Pensom was telling the truth the place might be bugged and their voices could have alerted listeners who might arrive at any time, and then it could be a really tough situation. Samson was confident he could look after himself but he didn't wish to carry a passenger who detested physical violence. He went to the second bedroom and examined the mirror. It was set into the wall and immediately above a wash-basin; traces of fresh grouting lined its perimeter. Moving fast for a big man he went to the airing cupboard which adjoined the room. He spotted a chewing gum wrapper on the floor.

'Do you ever chew gum?'

'Chew gum? No.'

'Right. Let's get out of here.'

'What do . . .'

Samson grabbed Pensom's arm and hauled him to the front door. Outside, he said, 'For the time being I'm suspending disbelief and going along with your story.' He hustled Pensom along a corridor and then stopped as he heard the whirr of the elevator on its way up. 'Is there some place to hide? A caretaker's closet or something?'

Pensom pointed to a door. 'That's a broom cupboard.'

'It'll do.' Samson thrust his uncomprehending client forward. 'Get inside. There isn't much room. You'll have to put up with physical contact.'

He left the door slightly ajar. The elevator stopped and its gates opened. Footsteps stopped close to number fourteen. A man's voice said, 'Try this one. It should fit.' Samson peered out. He was just in time to see two men

151

entering the flat.

On his own he would have used the opportunity for a show-down but Pensom was too much of an encumbrance. 'Come on,' he said, 'we're getting out fast.'

Pensom ran with him to the elevator. As it descended to the ground floor Samson said, 'If it's any comfort, I accept your story. No need for a psychiatrist.'

'As a matter of fact when I saw the flat had been restored I began to doubt you. I wondered if you'd been caught up in the plot and agreed to take me there for another surprise.'

The elevator stopped. 'Through the back,' said Samson as Pensom instinctively turned to go out through the front door. 'Unless our driver's a villain, he'll be waiting for us. And if he is a villain, I've got his cab number.'

The driver was behind the wheel reading a book on teach-yourself Spanish.

As they travelled back towards Battersea Samson said, 'I want you to keep a low profile. Only go out when you have to. And keep an eye on Vestier. From what little I know of his discretion I wouldn't trust him with a used matchstick.'

'OK. What are you going to do?'

Samson raised his eyebrows as though the question surprised him. 'I'm going to do what I've been going to do all along. Bring your case to a satisfactory conclusion.'

'You've got a plan?'

'Mr Pensom, any plans I have I keep to myself. Not that you would shout them from the rooftops but under pressure you might.'

Pensom's body posture changed. He shifted away from Samson and curves of relaxation became sharp angles. 'I'm not a coward, if that's what you think. I didn't cave in when I was trapped in that juggernaut. You've rubbed in the fact that I don't like physical contact but if it was a matter of life and death I wouldn't hesitate.' He paused and with bitterness in his voice added, 'I'm not a wimp.'

152

'Fine,' said Samson.

The taxi weaved through traffic, braked suddenly and the driver shouted at a motor-cyclist who'd tried to cut him up. '*Vaya! Tenemos prisa!*'

The cyclist acknowledged this information with a two-fingered insult.

'And *cojones* to you, mate,' bawled the driver.

Pensom went white. 'Bloody cyclist. That could have caused an accident. They ought to be banned.'

'But we didn't have an accident,' Samson pointed out, 'and our driver had the chance to practise his Spanish.'

'I know. My nerves are a bit on edge. I've been thinking. Have you heard of snuff movies, Mr Samson?'

'Yes.'

'Suppose Marler is behind all this and plans the film to end in a horrifying way with my death. Those two men might have been executioners.'

Samson laughed, not because he was amused, but in an attempt to lighten Pensom's mood. 'Nothing of the sort,' he said. 'That just wouldn't make sense.'

'Not to a normal person, but to someone with a warped mind. The execution of the generals who plotted against Hitler was filmed and he used to watch the film over and over again. And there was Beria of the KGB who used to have prostitutes snatched from the streets and tortured to death. Their death agonies were filmed and shown to a selected circle of friends.'

'Comfort yourself with the thought that you're neither a general nor a prostitute,' said Samson, 'and that Hitler and Beria are both dead. Stay indoors and I'll report back to you as soon as I can.'

Samson arrived back at his office via the fire escape. Although fairly fit for his size and weight he felt tired and then he remembered he still hadn't eaten since the brief low-calorie intake called breakfast. 'What's in the fridge?'

he asked as he opened the door.

Shandy hurriedly put down the phone.

'Private call or business?' Samson asked.

'Private, of course. When you're out I spend all my time chatting with friends. Why do you think your bill is so high?'

Samson gave a sour look. He didn't appreciate this sort of joke. In fact, he didn't regard it as a joke.

'There's some cold beef in the fridge, but most people eat less in hot weather. And anyway, that's for your lunch. No snacks inbetween.'

'This is an exception . . . What are you grinning at?'

'You. You've clambered up the fire escape when you could have come in at the front.'

'Explain.'

Shandy gave a demure look through long eyelashes. 'Shall I get the beef first, sir, or make the explanation?'

'Don't aggravate me. I'm not in the mood. I've just been pacifying a very nervous client. What's the explanation?'

'I checked with the estate agents and, what do you think, the council are at last going to do something about the street. They've got sick of environmentalists, parents' groups, road-safety campaigners, et cetera. They might, repeat might, install a light-controlled pedestrian crossing down the way by Patel's shop.'

'Shandy, come to the point, please.'

'Well, the agents have let the council use the place opposite to take a census and film traffic flow. We're not being spied on.'

'Good. Coffee with the beef, by the way.' Samson moved towards his room.

'Don't you want to hear what's gone on while you've been away?'

'Not until I've had refreshment.'

Samson went through the inter-connecting doorway and wandered across to the window. In the building opposite a man with a clipboard appeared to be making notes. Samson was so accustomed to street noise that he hardly noticed it, but now he realised that the volume of traffic was very heavy and when a child darted across the street, taking advantage of a temporary traffic standstill, he decided it would be no bad thing to install a proper crossing. Having convinced himself on this he had no further reason to avoid thinking about his current problem. The next logical step was to tackle GLJ, confront him with the evidence, and ask what the hell he was playing at. This might mean going north to Humberside or, if GLJ was in London with Gerda Vogel, finding out the address of his Mayfair flat.

Samson was acquainted with a lady who conducted business in an apartment near Shepherd Market. In her profession she ranked as 'high class' and she liked to call her customers 'clients'. She had a maid, a young Irish girl, whose wardrobe included gymslip, leather gear, nun's habit, and nurses' and policewomen's uniforms. It was possible that either of these ladies might be able to help with GLJ's address but, failing this, he could resort to door-to-door enquiries.

Shandy knocked and entered. Two thin slices of cold roast beef nestled on a plate decked with chives, lettuce, tomato and a spoonful of coleslaw. Next to this, on a tray, was a flask of coffee and a cup.

Samson rubbed his hands. 'Good. This should see me through till lunch.'

'This *is* your lunch.'

'We'll see. Now then, tell me what excitements you had while I was out. Does someone want a pet hamster found? Has that nutty dowser been offering his services again as an aid to detection?'

'Nothing as exciting as that. Just a phone call from a man calling himself Geraint Lloyd Jackson. I'm sure it wasn't important.'

Samson jerked forward in his chair. 'Why didn't you tell

155

me when I got in?'

'I tried to,' replied Shandy sweetly, 'but you insisted on being fed first.'

'All right. What did he want?'

'To meet you. He left a number for you to call back.'

'Did he say why he wanted to meet me?'

'No.' She lifted the flask and poured his coffee. 'Do you want me to get him now or wait until you've assuaged hunger pangs?'

'Eat first, work later, has been my motto since a poverty-stricken childhood.'

'Bring in the violins.'

'I'll let you know when I'm ready. Is it a London number?'

'Yes.'

'Fine. I didn't fancy going north. In fact I don't feel like moving from here. Too hot. Mohammed will have to come to the mountain.'

'Mountain is the *mot juste*,' said Shandy and made a fast exit.

'Mr Lloyd Jackson?'

'Speaking.'

'John Samson here.'

'Thanks for calling. I want to see you.'

'You want my professional services? A discreet enquiry perhaps?'

'No. I want to talk about a client of yours.'

'Sorry. Clients' business is strictly confidential.'

A breath of exasperation came down the line. 'If I told you your client's name was Pensom, would that make a difference?'

'It might. What do you want to talk about?'

'I can't tell you on the phone. I have a table booked at the Hilton for one o'clock. Can you join me there? It'll just be the two of us.'

'Sorry, Mr Lloyd Jackson, if you want to meet me you must come here.'

A long pause.

'Very well. What time?'

'Twelve noon?'

'Right.'

'You know my address?'

'I do.'

'Will you be coming by taxi?'

'Private car. I have a chauffeur.'

'Then tell him to allow extra time. The traffic here is chaotic. And there's nowhere to park.'

'Mr Samson, it would make much more sense for you to come to the Hilton. Your expenses will be met.'

'Thank you for the lunch offer but if we are to meet at all it must be here, in my office. And speaking of expenses, mine will be thirty pounds, provided our meeting doesn't last longer than an hour.'

Another hiss of exasperation came down the line. Then, 'I'll be there. Goodbye.'

The line went dead.

A moment later Shandy appeared. 'I was listening in. Not like you to turn down a free meal. Well done.'

'It hurt.'

'You were taking a chance asking him to come here *and* pay for your time.'

'Not really. He wouldn't have contacted me unless he badly wanted something from me, and wanting something badly always has a price.'

She looked at his empty plate. 'I might as well take the tray. Was it good?'

'Delicious. You're a gem, Shandy.'

She picked up the tray. 'I'm getting out. I don't trust your compliments. You're usually after something, like working late, or a pay cut.'

Samson regarded her rapid retreat with a fond gaze.

157

SOME PREDATORS ARE MALE

Part 6

Lloyd Jackson's face might have been carved out of Dakota rock. He was short in stature and walked as if his shoulders had been pinned back and attached by steel bands to a spinal rod. He wore an open-necked tartan-check shirt, faded blue jeans and white training shoes. He spoke with a mid-Atlantic accent and his first words were, 'I guess you know who I am.'

Standing behind his desk Samson indicated an assortment of chairs. 'Take a seat, Mr Jackson.'

'They have air-conditioning in the Hilton,' said Lloyd Jackson, selecting a chair with worn leather-studded seat and placing it close to Samson's desk and directly in front of him. He sat down and wiped his face with a tissue which, after use, he held in his hand as he looked around.

'Waste-paper basket?' enquired Samson. 'Here.'

Lloyd Jackson deposited the tissue.

Samson waited. The two men established eye contact and Samson continued to wait. He knew that if one looks at a point between another person's eyes a staring match can continue indefinitely. It was Lloyd Jackson who spoke first. 'I could use a glass of water. Tall, with ice.'

Samson buzzed Shandy and delivered the request.

Lloyd Jackson leaned slightly forward as if about to impart a confidence. 'I'm in television. Neil Pensom is working on a project with me.'

'What project is that?'

'I'll tell you. A thriller serial about diamond smuggling.'

161

'Diamond smuggling!' exclaimed Samson. 'That's original. I don't know where you chaps get your ideas from. Is it a good script?'

'That hasn't been finalised. Mr Samson, I will be entirely frank with you. In addition to the smuggling story, we are using Neil on another project although he doesn't realise this. Not yet. He will, though, and it will be greatly to his advantage. In the meanwhile, and until the time is right to reveal everything, it's essential he stays ignorant of the role he's playing. If it gets leaked everything will be spoiled. He wouldn't get his just and deserved remuneration.'

'Just and deserved remuneration,' Samson repeated slowly. 'That sounds very altruistic, Mr Jackson. Commercial television obviously has honourable ideals.'

Lloyd Jackson shifted in his seat and looked less than super self-assured. 'Well, yes. But we have to look to our own interests too. That's why I'm here.'

'What role is Mr Pensom playing in your secondary project?' Samson asked.

'That's the difficulty. If I tell you, and you tell him, and the word gets out, or if he freezes, gets self-conscious or stage fright, the whole thing goes up the spout. It's vital that he stays ignorant of his role until the shooting is finished.'

'You make it sound like Candid Camera,' said Samson.

Lloyd Jackson gave him a piercing look. 'You are either very smart or a lucky guesser.'

'Luck doesn't often come my way, so it must be the other thing you said.'

'Can I rely on your total confidentiality?'

'No.'

'No! Jesus Christ, do you want your client to make a fat profit or get fired? Those are the options. Believe me, I could have him fired tomorrow. And he wouldn't stand a chance of getting similar employment elsewhere. I'd see to that. He's a liability. He cost my company thousands on our last project. Has he told you about it?'

'He may have. But I'd like to hear your version.'

'The story was about a guy who commandeered a Mosquito aircraft after it had been performing at an air display. He took this aircraft and flew it all over the place just one jump ahead of the police. He threatened to bomb Buckingham Palace. Neil's job was to line up an old airfield in East Anglia. He didn't do the job properly. One of the airfields was owned by a farmer and Neil didn't get a written clearance permitting us to use it. He thought the guy was an agricultural farmer and was content with an oral agreement from someone calling himself a farm manager. Only he wasn't a farm manager, and it wasn't an agricultural farm. It was a mink farm. The mink were scared out of breeding by the low-flying aircraft and we were taken to the cleaners. Or would have been if we hadn't settled out of court.'

While he was speaking Samson noticed that the hour-glass on his desk needed turning. He had leaned forward and turned it. It was an act of calculated inattentiveness.

'Were you listening to me, Mr Samson?'

'Yes.'

'Great. I wouldn't want to pay you thirty pounds for the privilege of talking to myself.'

'Did Eva Grunblatt tell you I was an expert on timepieces when she sent you my photograph?'

The shadow of a smile crossed Lloyd Jackson's rock-like face. 'No, she told me on the phone.'

'And you sent a camera-man to Heathrow to film me.'

Lloyd Jackson's smile came into full sunlight. 'Boy, did you make a mistake there! You roughed up a total stranger. My man watched it all and sent in his girlfriend to break it up. Just as well she came on the scene or that poor guy might have been crippled for life.'

163

'You hadn't had my photo then?'

'Not yet. You were identified as soon as you came through customs. Eva had given a good description and there aren't many like you.'

Samson took the inference stoically. 'Your man tailed me to my home?'

'That's right. And when we found out your job we guessed it was Neil who'd hired you. We also guessed he'd hired you to find out what was going on. Right?'

'Maybe.'

'You outsmarted us today. Twice. We missed you leaving your office and we missed you by a whisker at Neil's apartment in Dulwich. That's why I'm here. I can't contact Neil so I have to get your goodwill and the only way to do that, or so I reckon, is to put all my cards on the table.'

'Including the one up your sleeve?'

Lloyd Jackson looked injured. 'That's a cheap remark.'

'Cheap it may be,' said Samson, 'but I resent the way my client has been hounded and deprived of the comfort of his home. You've got a lot of explaining to do. But before you begin, as a matter of interest, what did you mean when you said I was missed when I left the office this morning. Did you have someone watching?'

'Sure I did. When I knew where you hung out business-wise I hired the place opposite and installed a camera.'

From under heavy-lidded eyes Samson glanced sideways and down to check that his concealed tape-recorder was operating and, as he did so, he said, 'I'd heard that it was a council scheme to monitor traffic flow.'

'That was the line I gave the estate agents and they swallowed it.'

'And all in the interests of my client getting his just and deserved remuneration. Amazing. Now tell me what this is all about.'

'I'd sure like to, but I do need your undertaking that it won't go any further. If it did, everything could be fouled up.'

'The only undertaking I'll give is that I won't inform your rival companies.'

Lloyd Jackson sighed. 'I guess that'll have to do. You could say it all began in the sixties when everything was still in black and white. There was a weekly Candid Camera programme. It featured Jonathan Routh, Liz Reber and others. I thought it was terrific but wondered how the people felt when they found they'd been fooled. I discovered they didn't mind at all. And they were always paid. That made it all right. The film-makers couldn't be prosecuted. Payment prevents prosecution. Do you know how much they got paid for their unscripted appearances?'

'I've no idea.'

'Ten shillings. Fifty pence in today's money. It was worth more then but still peanuts. Anyway, I got to wondering what it would be like to have a full-length feature made of someone in that situation rather than three-minute shorts. Over the years I played with the idea and then the opportunity came. Neil went to pieces after his mother died. I thought it would do him good to get him out of himself if he was made a mark. The alternative was to fire him for incompetence. I didn't want the guy to be fired on top of losing his mother.'

'Altruism indeed,' Samson remarked.

'I hope you meant that sincerely, Mr Samson, because I was sincere. I like Neil but he has to go. But he can go with a fat handshake if I can complete the film.'

A rap on the door and Shandy entered with a lager glass filled with iced water. 'Sorry I've been so long but I got held up. . . . Mr Samson, Lady W would like you to contact her as soon as possible. His lordship is threatening proceedings. I told her you were in conference.'

165

Samson frowned and looked very serious. Nobody would have guessed that inwardly he was quivering with suppressed laughter. Shandy was adept at turning her faults to advantage. She had either forgotten about the water or been delayed by a call from a friend and the rubbish about Lady W was not only a cover but was intended to impress Lloyd Jackson.

Samson reached for a pad and made a note. 'Right,' he said. 'I'll call as soon as I'm free.' When Shandy had left the room he pushed the notepad aside and looked across his desk at Lloyd Jackson. 'You were speaking of completing the film. What was to come next? After the seduction in his own flat.'

Lloyd Jackson held up his hand. 'Just a minute. I don't know what went on under the covers. And anyway, it may be edited out. I may not use the British agent bit either.'

'I must say it struck me as being out of key, but I'm not artistic. I repeat, what was to come next?'

'The next scene?'

'Yes.'

'The arrival of Amanda claiming they were married in a registry office. This started fine but then Neil made his escape just when Amanda was going to say she'd got a parson to come along and he'd be there any minute to bless their union. And there would be other wedding guests. Felicity's sisters. I heard Neil raced past them as they were getting out of the elevator. He missed something. All the girls were going to claim to be masseuses and offer a free massage to relax him for the blessing.'

'It sounds nightmarish.'

'It would have made a great scene. The audience would have loved it. They still could if we finish the shooting. I suppose they still could if we could persuade Neil to co-operate and act the part. Trouble is he might act twitchy and not be natural twitchy and the difference would show.' He paused to drink water. 'Another thing. Problems of

166

presentation. Would we go ahead on the basis that Neil knew nothing of what was going on from beginning to end and finish, as planned, with the filmed revelation to him and his amazed reaction? Or would we come clean and say that half-way through Neil found out what was happening but agreed to complete the film? That sounds feeble. Kiss of death. But if we do fake the ending, and it's blown, no distributor will take it.'

'Those are your problems,' said Samson with an edge of malicious pleasure in his voice, 'and you brought them on yourself.'

'Thanks a lot.'

'How does Marler fit into all this?'

'Marler?'

Samson reckoned he could tell a genuine from a feigned reaction, and truth from a lie, and Lloyd Jackson seemed honestly foxed by the question about Marler.

'He belongs to your golf club, the Swanley Bar,' said Samson.

Understanding flooded the crags of Lloyd Jackson's face. 'Oh, Tom Marler! I know him. Nice guy. What's he got to do with my project?'

'That's what I'm asking you.'

Lloyd Jackson was still plainly baffled. 'I'm not sure what you're driving at but if it's that Tom's bank is backing me your ball has landed in the rough.'

'Tom's bank?' queried Samson. 'Is Tom a banker as "banker" in roulette?'

Lloyd Jackson gave a snort of derision. 'You have to be joking. He's a manager with the Midland. Has a fifteen handicap. Very popular. Tells some great jokes.'

'Lives in Guernsey?' asked Samson.

'Ah, that's an unhappy story. His wife is overly concerned for her health. You could call her hypochondriac. She insisted the climate in the Channel Islands would be good for her. So they moved there, but it didn't work out. The expense and commuting problems. So Tom lives over here now and she lives there. But what the hell has Tom to do with this?'

Samson sighed. 'Nothing, it seems. 'He's the wrong Marler.'

'While we're at it, how come you know about my club?'

'Investigative enquiries.'

'If I find your so-called investigative enquiries have in any way smeared my reputation you'll be stung, and stung hard.'

'They haven't. If you're not being backed by bank manager Marler, or any other Marler, who is backing you?'

'That isn't your business, but since I need your co-operation I'm prepared to tell you. I am my own backer. All my own money and done on a shoestring. The parts are being played mostly by friends for expenses only with the promise of a small slice of any net profits. The professionals employed are doing it cheap. OK? But' – Lloyd Jackson paused for effect – 'if Neil participates fully he will be on to a percentage of the *gross*.'

'How do Equity and the other unions feel about that?'

'I'll meet that problem when it comes. You have to appreciate that the fewer who know about this, the better. Any publicity now is bad news. Publicity when I'm ready will be maximised.'

Samson pondered. 'I'd guess my client wouldn't want publicity.'

'That's for him. When he hears the generosity of my offer and knows he's finished with Humberside he may be realistic.' Lloyd Jackson sat back. 'How about it, Mr Samson? You going to do your client a good turn and advise him to co-operate?'

'I'll think about it.'

'Think about it! Jesus Christ, I hope you will.' He glanced around the room. 'I don't know what value your

168

clocks have to a collector, but their functional value is zilch. Not one of the damn things is going. Well, my time hasn't stopped. Every wasted day is costing me money.' He took a deep breath in visible self-control. 'I'll make you an offer. Three thousand in cash if you'll tell me where Neil is and keep your mouth shut.'

'Bribery?'

'Bribery nothing. A mutually profitable business proposition which benefits your client. You make money, I buy time, and Neil comes out in the end with a fat bonus. Everyone is happy.'

Samson slowly shook his head from side to side as if responding to the measured beat of a metronome set at largo. He said nothing.

'OK then,' said Lloyd Jackson, doing his best to seem unconcerned, 'we'll play it your way. Will you give me a call as soon as you've thought it over?'

'Certainly.'

'I'll hold everything till I hear from you.'

Samson didn't believe him but said, 'A wise decision. I'll be in touch as soon as I can but something needs clarifying first.'

'What's that?'

'You mentioned a fat bonus if participation is agreed?'

'Sure. A cash sum and a share in the gross profits.'

'And if he doesn't participate?'

Lloyd Jackson gave the sort of thin smile Samson had been practising a couple of days earlier. 'That's his loss.'

'Wrong,' said Samson. 'It'll be your loss. You'll have an injunction slapped on you to prevent the showing of the film in any shape or form and there'll be a claim for damages for libel. It's not up to me to advise my client to go along with your plans; it's up to you to revise your budget to allow for costs should my client take legal action against you.'

Lloyd Jackson erupted. 'I don't have to take this sort of

169

shit from you.'

'You do. You're over a barrel. But if you call off your watchdogs over the road, don't put tails on me, and stop trying to locate my client. I'll put your proposition to him. Even-handedly. But if he or I get the slightest aggravation from you I guarantee your film will never be completed or shown.'

Lloyd Jackson had the ability to switch off anger. One moment he looked about to turn into volcanic lava, the next he was as impassive as Gibralter. After a pause he said, 'I accept. I'll comply for forty-eight hours. After that, I can't predict what might happen.'

'Is that a threat, Mr Jackson?'

'Heaven forbid, Mr Samson.'

'How much are you offering as a fat bonus?'

'Ten thousand, but it's a negotiable figure. And there would be a proper contract, legal and binding.'

Samson nodded. 'Before you go I've got one or two more questions, but they're only incidental to the main issue.'

'Shoot.'

'When Mr Pensom was dumped by his kidnappers he was given cryptic clues on his whereabouts. The architect can see his masterpiece on a clear day and something about the dock area in Antwerp. I can't see the point of mysterious clues.'

'It was an idea I had, but I've scrapped it. A combination of Candid Camera and Treasure Hunt. You can't mix the two; if you try, both could fall flat.'

'What about the police and customs officials? Were they genuine?'

'No.'

'And Neil Pensom was deliberately allowed to escape by Herr Vogel?'

'That's right. The situation had been milked. It was time for him to go back to his flat and the next scene.'

'I see. And has the film got a title?'

'Only a working title. I was going to give it the working title of *The Chase* but someone in the crew who's into psychology suggested *Vagina Dentata*. When he explained it we had a laugh and decided to use it, but, I emphasise, as a working title only.'

'I like *The Chase* much better,' said Samson, who had a prudish streak. Reflectively he added, '*The Chase* is good. It's a universal truth that most predators are female.'

'Right.'

'But some predators are male.'

'Meaning me, Mr Samson?'

'If the cap fits.'

'Predators have victims. I don't have victims. Neil is no victim.'

'I doubt if he'd agree.' Samson pressed a concealed button and stood up. Shandy entered. 'Show Mr Jackson out will you, my dear.' He extended his hand. 'Good day, Mr Jackson. You can either pay my secretary now, or I'll send you my account, whichever you prefer.'

After a moment's hesitation Lloyd Jackson shook hands. 'Bill me,' he said.

When Shandy returned Samson told her what had taken place at the interview, excluding the working title but including the final comments about predators. He did it to tease, expecting her to assert indignantly that the female predator was a myth invented by men but he misjudged her reaction.

'You're absolutely right,' she said. 'Poor Paul didn't stand a chance once I'd set my sights on him.' She tipped her head to one side and gave her boss a curious look. 'You don't fit into either category, predator or victim.'

'I'm in the third category. The one that needs both predators and victims in order to survive.' He gave a sad smile. 'I'm a mere scavenger.'

171

'Oh, bring back those violins! Anyway, what's the next move?'

Samson went over to the window. 'A pedestrian crossing down there is a good idea. I think I'll take up the matter with the highway authority.'

Shandy, knowing the way his mind worked, realised he wasn't ready to answer her question and the remark about the crossing was a means of playing for time. Above the noise of street traffic came the strident klaxoning of an ambulance. Its alarm had passed and faded before Samson spoke.

'I'd assumed that Marler's demands had stopped because he was involved with Jackson in this film. The timing seemed right for this. But if Marler isn't associated with Jackson, why has he stopped making demands?' He turned away from the window to face Shandy.

'I've no idea,' she said.

'I wonder,' Samson began, and paused for so long that Shandy felt obliged to ask, 'What do you wonder?'

'Tell you later. Would you get me a line? No, I'll get it myself in case that prying old man answers.'

Mystified, Shandy left the room.

Samson dialled a number.

'John Samson here. A quick call. Who handled your mother's estate?'

'Mother's estate? I don't follow you.'

'Never mind. Who?'

'Arkwright, Bottomley and Roker. They're an old-established firm of solicitors.'

'Were you executor of her will?'

'No. And that upset me. Not long before she died Mother made a new will making different provisions and appointing Mr Roker and a junior partner the executors and trustees. But why do you want to know?'

'What's your relationship with Roker like? Good, indifferent, bad?'

172

'Not good. Not good at all. I let him know how I felt about Mother's will being changed. I reckon he must have used undue influence. I went to another lawyer and took independent advice. I was told I hadn't really got a leg to stand on. The charging clause in favour of Roker's firm was perfectly normal and he didn't personally benefit. I still don't understand why you want to know all this.'

'I'll come and see you later today,' said Samson, 'and then, hopefully, I'll be able to explain everything and put a proposition to you. Goodbye for now.'

The offices of Arkwright, Bottomley and Roker were close to Chancery Lane and the Law Courts. Normally Samson would have gone there by taxi but today he preferred to travel by public transport and on foot so as to make it easier for someone to follow him and therefore to check whether he was being followed. He was testing Lloyd Jackson's forty-eight-hour undertaking.

The heatwave which had made a giant sweat-box of London was beginning to break. A fleece of cloud had thickened into a grey blanket, and the air was oppressively still in the calm heralding a rainstorm, when Samson surfaced from the underground at Chancery Lane station. He bought a copy of the Standard from a newsvendor and looked around. So far as he could tell, nobody had followed him. Lloyd Jackson had kept his word. It remained to be seen whether J R Roker whose name appeared third on a list of twelve partners would be as co-operative.

The legal firm occupied a stately Georgian building which was listed as having historical interest and architectural merit. A warren of corridors lay behind the façade and Samson was conducted by a circuitous route to an office on the first floor. He entered a room which had its walls lined with bound law reports and statutes. Roker stood behind a document-littered mahogany table. He was a tall, well-built man of about fifty-five with sandy hair and a thick moustache. He spoke in a deep resonant voice which had often been projected across courtrooms. 'Take a seat, Mr Samson.'

Samson selected a chair large enough to accommodate his frame.

'Now then, what is this exceptionally urgent matter concerning my trusteeship of a will that also concerns you?'

Sitting back in his chair, fingertips pressed to fingertips, Roker looked and sounded like a judge demanding an explanation from a subpoenaed witness.

Taking his time, careful not to omit anything relevant, Samson told of his first interview with Neil Pensom and of the typescript detailing his unwanted adventures. As he went through the narrative Roker began to frown and the frown deepened until a vertical cleft appeared between his eyebrows. 'But this is intolerable!' he exclaimed. 'Why wasn't I consulted earlier? Or, if not me, some other solicitor? Did you advise against it?'

From this point his interruptions were continuous. He might have been interrogating someone who was an accessory before the fact of a crime. But Samson was undisturbed by the hostile attitude; he was accustomed to mistrust of his profession by lawyers. He explained quietly that the only advice he had offered was for Pensom to lie low until the mystery was solved. Only when it was known who was responsible could any constructive action be taken.

He continued with the story, weathering Roker's fierce interruptions, until finally he came to the point when he could have disclosed the identity of the person who had set up Neil Pensom as leading man in a tale of pursuit.

'And who is it?' asked Roker. 'I demand to know.'

'Mr Pensom is my client,' said Samson. 'Is he your client as well? Has he instructed you to act for him?'

174

Roker's frown was so intense that his eyebrows seemed knitted together. "I acted for his late mother. I am joint trustee of her estate.'

'Ah, yes. I was coming to that. Mr Pensom is under the impression that someone called Marler is behind it all.'

Roker abandoned the judge-like pose. He leaned forward, resting his arms on the table and his fists were clenched. At the mention of Marler's name something seemed to pass in front of Roker's eyes that he recognised and instantly dismissed.

'You know him?' asked Samson.

'I can't say I do. Is he responsible for Mr Pensom's troubles?'

'I'm not prepared to say who's responsible until I know the position re Mr Pensom's debts, and whether they have been paid off.'

Roker made a show of being taken aback. 'I don't follow the logic of that.'

'Perhaps not, but unless you can help me on the question of who paid off the debts I'm not in a position to tell you what I know.'

'And what makes you think I can help you? And what makes you think these alleged debts might have been paid off? Really, Mr Samson, I find your attempts to bargain with me unethical in the extreme.'

Samson remained unruffled. He knew the sound of fury signifying nothing when he heard it. 'You ask what makes me think you can help me. I will tell you. There is only one person who'd wish to pay off Mr Pensom's debts. His mother. I believe these debts have been paid off, because demands which were insistent and intimidating suddenly stopped. I know that Mr Pensom expected to be executor of his mother's will and was shaken when he learned that you and someone else had been appointed in his place by a new will. I don't know why she changed her mind about having

175

her son administer her estate, or why he was simply given a life interest on the income from the capital, but at a guess she didn't trust him not to fritter away everything in gambling.'

Samson looked hard at the man on the opposite side of the table who had begun the interview as an impartial judge but was now an adversary.

'I hope you don't expect me to discuss my late client's affairs,' said Roker loftily.

'Of course not. But it must have troubled her when she discovered he was a compulsive gambler and the extent of his debts.'

'Naturally.'

The moment he had spoken, Roker realised he had been bluffed into admitting that Neil Pensom's mother was aware of her son's debts. It was a critical moment. He could either harden his stance of non-co-operation or accept that he shared a common cause with Samson.

'I have a mind to terminate this meeting,' he said; 'I'm not sure what useful purpose it serves.'

'But your mind isn't a closed mind. At least, I hope it isn't.'

'No, I'm open to persuasion.'

The change of demeanour wasn't lost on Samson. When a lawyer announces he is open to persuasion it is a face-saving formula for not saying he's changed his mind or lost an argument.

'If it were to be the case,' he said, choosing his words with the caution of a man walking through a minefield, 'that the late Mrs Pensom knew of her son's weakness and made arrangements that debts should be honoured, but preferred he shouldn't know of her generosity so that he could maintain the belief that she was unaware of the weakness, then I would be the last one to inform him.'

Roker was no longer frowning and in his voice there was

a certain grudging respect. 'I like the way you said that. I'm not sure whether you know it, but Mrs Pensom was a very strong-willed woman. I wouldn't say domineering. That would be wrong. But she was dominant in all her relationships. She knew gambling debts were legally unenforceable but also she knew certain men would stop at nothing. Moreover, she knew something her son didn't – that her days were numbered. She changed her will and made arrangements with me to set aside a sum to meet the debts. Shortly afterwards she died. I have done what she wished and obtained a written discharge as well as the return of the IOUs. It was her wish that Neil should never be told that she knew of his debts or that she had repaid them. Do I have your word that you'll respect her wish and keep what I've told you in the strictest confidence?'

'You have my word,' said Samson.

'Now tell me who's behind this exploitation of a man to make what I believe is known as "good box-office"? If it's Marler, I shall make sure he regrets it.'

'It's not Marler. But I'm not willing to name names. Not yet.'

'Not yet!' Roker was incredulous.

'You mentioned ethics earlier. It wouldn't be ethical for me to tell you until I've informed my client and consulted with him.'

Roker made a noise like a suppressed growl. 'Mr Samson, I don't know whether to respect your integrity or dismiss you as a sharp operator.'

Samson gave his widest smile. 'Can't I be both?' he asked. 'A sharp operator with integrity?' Sensing he had outstayed a negligible welcome he stood up. He took a card from his wallet. 'This is my card. Please send a note of your fee for this consultation to my office. And if you should need the sort of service I provide, I should be happy to oblige.'

* * *

He called Shandy from a public call-box. After telling her of the outcome of his interview with Roker he asked if she had anything to report.

'Only that our watchers have gone. They left about half an hour ago.'

'Good. I'm on my way to see Pensom. See you later.'

He went by taxi to the apartment block where Pensom was in hiding. This time he arrived at the front and after paying the driver hurried to the entrance. Rain was streaking down from a heavy bank of cloud and bouncing off the asphalt forecourt. Pensom answered the entry-phone and soon Samson was back in the chaos of Anthony Vestier's spare room, once more seated on the anvil.

While Pensom listened dumbfounded Samson gave a résumé of his meeting with Lloyd Jackson. He concluded, 'It's up to you what you do.'

'I'm staggered. . . . I don't know what to think. . . .'

Samson sat quietly while Pensom spoke in disjointed phrases. He wasn't surprised that Pensom should be shaken but thought it odd that, rather than considering whether to go along with Lloyd Jackson's project or to take legal action against him, Pensom seemed preoccupied with the brilliance of Eva Grunblatt's acting.

'At one stage I began to wonder whether she was telling the truth and I'd lost my memory. Maybe I really was married to her. . . . Incredible. . . . The relentless pursuit by a female, you say?' He laughed. 'She played that part to perfection. I've been thinking about her since your last visit. It's not easy to imagine her without that mole. . . .'

Eventually Samson interrupted with, 'There's something else I must tell you.'

Pensom pulled himself together. 'I'll have to think over GLJ's proposition, of course. But I do need the money. The point is . . .'

Samson held up his hand in a silencing gesture. 'Just a

178

moment. Hear what I've got to say. You are immune to threats from Marler. You have nothing to fear from that quarter. There are no debts to be paid off.'

'No debts? What do you mean?'

'They were repaid by an anonymous friend.'

'I don't believe it. It can't be.'

'It is.'

Pensom, who had been seated, jumped to his feet and went to the door. He opened it suddenly, checking whether anyone was listening outside. Satisfied there was no eavesdropper he returned to the bar-stool and, in a lowered voice, asked, 'It wasn't Anthony, was it? I've always suspected he's better off than he pretends.'

'It wasn't Anthony and that's the last bit of information you'll get.'

'How did you find this out?'

'The donor must remain anonymous. Leave it at that.'

A silence opened between them. From an adjoining room the faint strains of Beethoven's fifth symphony could be heard.

Pensom spoke first. 'Anthony is a bit deaf. The radio is always on at full volume. Luckily we share the same tastes in music.'

'Will you be staying on here?' Samson asked.

'No need now, is there?. . . . Am I really off the hook with Marler?'

'Off the hook completely.'

A look of enormous relief spread over Pensom's face and he seemed to relax inside his clothes. 'So all I have to do is decide what to do about GLJ's proposition?'

'That's right.' Samson stood up. 'This winds up the case as far as I'm concerned, but if there's anything more I can do, let me know.'

'I'm very grateful. It still hasn't quite sunk in yet.'

Pensom got to his feet and moved towards the door. Before

opening it he asked, 'What would you do?'

'What would I do if I were in your shoes?'

'Yes.'

'I'd contact Jackson and ask exactly what he would offer if I agreed to carry on with the film and ask him to let me have it in writing. Then I'd negotiate for the best terms possible and get a lawyer to vet the contract. Good luck.'

Samson sent his account to Pensom's own address and received a cheque in payment by return. It came with a note, 'I've decided to go ahead with the project even though GLJ wants it to end with a fake wedding between Eva and me!'

Some weeks passed and then one morning, when Shandy brought in the mail, she said, 'I haven't opened this one. It's marked "Very personal".'

Samson slit open the envelope, read the letter, laughed, and handed it to Shandy.

Dear Mr Samson,

The film is almost completed. Only the wedding scene remains to be shot. But it isn't to be a fake wedding! It will be for real! Eva and I are getting married. I know you will find this hard to understand in view of what I wrote in the script I gave you but she isn't at all like the part she had to play. We found we got along marvellously when we were able to be ourselves and were not being manipulated into impossible situations.

I have been back to Steinbach to stay with her and we and the Vogels have had some good laughs about the night I was 'forced' to spend with her. She teases me dreadfully about the fact that I was willing to climb into bed with Felicity Flowerdew (not her real name, by the way) and yet resisted Eva's overtures! I've told her that nothing much actually happened but I'm not sure she believes me. Anyway, that scene is to be cut from the film.

180

The wedding is due to take place on 12 October at the Hampstead Registry Office. It is planned to have about twenty guests present although there will be many more at the reception. But the object of this letter isn't simply to tell you my news but also to ask if you would be one of the wedding guests. GLJ says there will be no payment for the extras in this scene which strikes me as a bit mean but he's on a very tight budget. I do hope you can come.

Sincerely yours,
Neil Pensom

'And will you go?' Shandy asked.

'In my job, as you know,' said Samson, 'there are few happy endings. Yes, I shall go.' As an afterthought, and more to himself than Shandy, he added, 'I'd like to be part of a happy ending, even if it's someone else's.'